Hidden Sins

Alison Joseph

Chapter One

There was a sharpness in the wind, in spite of the blue of the sky, the sparkle of the sea. Agatha Christie took careful steps along the cliff-top track, thinking about true love. The kind in books, she thought, as her brown brogues scuffed the yellow-flowering gorse.

And in real life?

That morning, her husband had held her in his arms and mumbled a goodbye, the little Cornish railway station all noise and steam, glimpses of lace ironwork amidst the heaped luggage, the harassed nannies, the bright chatter of children.

'London,' Archie was saying, 'business, office, only a few days, you'll have a wonderful time, new book, getting on with it, peace and quiet, sea air, soon be back with me...'

Something like that.

Agatha gazed out at the white-flecked ocean.

I love you. That's what people say in books. The hero takes hold of the heroine's hands and says, 'I love you.'

But only at the story's end.

She turned away from the cliff and rejoined the path, the June sun on her face as she descended the hill. My new book, she thought. A romance. The characters had begun to take shape. A Captain, a brave, military type. A shy but clever young woman, destined to marry someone dull, someone chosen by her mother, a well-meaning but fearful woman who worries for her daughter's future…

But my readers will know, thought Agatha, that the brave Captain and the shy young woman need to be together.

'A romance?' Archie had said, a week or so ago when she'd first mentioned it. It had been at home, at dinner, during several days of constant rain. 'Are you sure?'

She'd looked at him across the silverware.

'The detective stuff is doing so well,' he'd said.

'I've got this idea…' she'd said.

His face fixed, tightened.

'I thought I'd work on it when we're in Cornwall,' she'd said.

'It's supposed to be a holiday,' he'd said, picking up his fork.

Now, alone, she walked towards the village. After three days, Archie had decided two things; one, that the golf course here was really quite sub-standard compared to the one at home, 'bumps and dips everywhere, and then that sea view, and trying to land your drive on to the green with that blustery wind, what do they expect a chap to do? If their golf facilities were half as good as their tennis courts I might be tempted to stay…' And secondly, that the office really couldn't do without him any longer.

This morning she had let him go, a hurried goodbye in the midst of smoke and slamming doors.

I love you, people say in books.

I love you, my Captain will say to my shy young woman.

It will be the end of the story.

Her thoughts were interrupted by loud shouts, and laughter, as she rounded the corner and the coastal village came into view, no more than a scattering of cottages. The tide was out, and on the sands a group of people stood clustered around a structure, dark and jagged-edged against the shining sea. The curves of a prow, she saw, the ruins of a shipwreck. They seemed to be working on it, and now she could hear hammering, and every so often a small group broke away and carried part of the structure towards the shore.

So this is the *Lady Leona*, she thought. Little May at the hotel had told her all about it this morning, sitting at reception with her tub of silver polish. 'It's an old fishing boat,' she'd said. 'Hit the rocks, been there for a year and a day. More than that, in fact. So now it means that the wreckers can help themselves. It's the law, see? And with these low spring tides, they've decided to haul her in, to see what she holds. They say they'll find gold.' She'd giggled, with a shake of her pretty curls. 'Dead fish, more like. That's what I think anyways. And ghosts. Loads of ghosts. The dead, see. They don't like to be disturbed.' She'd laughed again, and returned to the candlesticks.

Agatha's gaze went to the activity beneath them on the sands, the strong young men in rough shirts hauling huge, barnacled ribs of wood, the women kneeling, digging at the hulk, or standing, watching, the sea breeze catching at their shawls. The whole scene reflected blue and gold on the tide-washed sands.

5

Ghosts, she thought. It had occurred to her that her Captain would have a sense of being haunted, something to do with a war, not the war just gone, not that, no — an earlier war, one of glory and horsemanship, of etiquette and justice.

Not the war just gone.

It changed us all, she thought, gazing downwards at the activity below. Hospital memories, again. A soldier shouting in pain, 'my leg, nurse, my leg, do something about my leg…' He'd grabbed her hand, tried to pull her towards his injured leg. 'Here, Nurse, it hurts so much…'

There is no leg, she'd wanted to say. I washed the operating theatre clean of your blood. That pain, is the ghost of your leg.

She turned away from the view of the ship. It was time to get back to the hotel. There will be afternoon tea, she thought. I will sit with my notebook. There will be cucumber sandwiches, and Darjeeling, and my brave Captain in his scarlet coat. He will wear medals, and ride to hounds. He'll be strong, and whole, and his hauntings will be the sort that can be cured.

She walked along the sandy track, thinking about her work, thinking about her solitary table in the Palm Court tea room. The hotel manager had suggested, now she was alone, that she might like to be placed with some of the other guests. There was a quiet couple, Mr. and Mrs. Collyer, the wife young, nervous and pretty, the husband somewhat older, balding, with a large moustache and a collection of rather loud checked jackets. There was an angular young man named Mr. Farrar, smart, clean-shaven and cigarette-smoking, who had arrived at the hotel a week or so before, in the company of a slightly older woman who seemed to be a relative, and her daughter, a quiet blonde girl of about fifteen who was always on the tennis courts. Agatha had noticed her repetitive practice, an odd mixture of boredom and obsession. A sporty young man called Sebastian Travers made up their party. He seemed to be the girl's tennis coach. He would engage her in all sorts of practice exercises, but the blank expression and the tightness in her shoulders seemed to stay the same. Then there was an older man, solitary, neat and polite, with a small moustache and a military air. He walked with a stick, and he tended to wear a white straw hat. He had a certain ease with the staff, as if he might be a regular guest.

Agatha began to ascend the hill away from the village. The prospect of solitude, of sandwiches and scones, was very appealing. She would sit alone, and think about what kind of ghost would be haunting her brave Captain.

Chapter Two

The afternoon sunlight dazzled on the white of the terrace. The sea view was azure, the tennis courts emerald green. Agatha chose a shady table, and took out her notebook. There was laughter from the tennis courts, as three youths, apparently local, were batting a ball to and fro. The young tennis girl was sitting by the courts, reading a book.

A dark-haired boy in kitchen whites appeared with a plate of cakes. Agatha saw the girl take one, and giggle, and the boy giggled too, before being called away by a matronly aproned woman, with a wag of her finger.

'May we join you?'

She looked up to see the moustached man in the loud checked jacket, his wife at his side. His wife began to speak – 'Frederick, I'm not sure she wants…' But the husband ignored her. 'Shame to see Mrs. Christie sitting all alone,' he said. 'And anyway, we thought we'd sit in the shade, didn't we, Nora?'

Agatha shifted her cup to one side, gestured to the two seats next to her.

'The sun is rather intrusive,' she said.

'We like it,' Mrs. Collyer said. She was wearing a pale tea-gown, patterned with tiny pink flowers, and her fine blonde hair was pinned up.

Her husband clattered his way to the shady chair.

'Are you enjoying your holiday?' Nora Collyer asked.

'Mr. Christie not here?' her husband interrupted.

'He had to go back to London,' Agatha said. 'His business...'

'Ah.' Mr. Collyer nodded.

There was a brief silence. Then the hotel manager, Mr. Finch, appeared at their side. He was in white, with a bow tie, short white-blonde hair and a crisp, upright demeanour.

'Tea, Sir?'

'Yes. For two. We'll have Earl Grey,' Mr. Hastings said.

'And anything to eat?'

'Oh no.' Mr. Collyer leaned back expansively in his chair. 'We'll be having dinner soon enough.'

Agatha noticed his wife eyeing the plate of cakes, but Mrs. Collyer said nothing.

'That's the problem with having an office,' Mr. Collyer said, conversationally. 'It's not a problem I have.'

'Oh?' Agatha realized she knew nothing about these two, other than that they had been at the hotel for almost a month already, and it was something to do with the husband's work.

'Writing a book, y'see,' Mr. Collyer said.

'Oh.'

'A major work of biography,' he went on. 'Foremost in its field, it'll be.'

She nodded, politely.

'You'll have heard of Ernst Adler, the well-known chemist?'

Agatha had to admit that, no, she hadn't.

He made a brief huffing noise. 'Well, perhaps in your world his fame hasn't yet spread. Surrey, isn't it?'

'Berkshire,' Agatha said. 'But –'

'Quite,' Mr. Collyer interrupted. 'Dr. Adler is a giant in his field. In my field too. I've always admired him, followed in his footsteps, y'see. Worked in the same branch of chemistry. Always promised him that I'd write his biography. Poor chap passed away two years ago now, and then I found myself without a lab, so I started on it. Been staying here every summer since then. His house is inland from here, mile or so from the village, his widow lives there still. Of course, she's delighted, nothing too much trouble for me, isn't she, dear?'

He nodded his head briefly towards his wife, who seemed to be about to speak, but then he continued, 'Cobalt salts, pigments, y'see. Essential right across the board. Dr. Adler worked on the stabilisation of sulphides, made the field what it is today –'

He stopped as Mr. Finch appeared with tea, and began to pour it. As the pot approached Mr. Collyer's cup, he raised his large hand.

'No no no. Milk in first.' His voice was harsh. 'Don't they teach you people anything? Changes the taste if you add the milk to the tea. I'll pour my own, thank you. Just leave the pot there.'

Mr. Finch inclined his head in acknowledgement, gave a brief nod to Mrs. Collyer and departed.

'Sugar tongs,' Mr. Collyer shouted after him. 'We don't seem to have any.'

10

Again, the tilt of the head, the quiet glide towards the kitchen.

'Only thing wrong with this place,' Mr. Collyer said. 'They just can't get the staff. I blame the war. Gave these sort of chaps ideas above their station.'

'It wouldn't be any different if we stayed anywhere else, dear,' Mrs. Collyer's gentle voice intervened. 'You complain wherever we go.' She spoke with equanimity, a warmth in her hazel eyes, her fingers fiddling with her necklace, which was a string of delicate beads in pink and green. Archie had remarked on Mrs. Collyer's elegance the first night they were there, and it was true, Agatha thought, that even if she'd been in military fatigues or chef's overalls she'd still look like something from a fashion magazine.

Beneath them on the tennis courts, the young girl had started a match with her coach. Her mother was standing on the side-lines, shouting encouragement in rather harsh terms.

'One does rather feel for that child,' Mrs. Collyer said. 'Sophie,' she added. 'Her mother, Mrs. Winters, claims she has a great talent, but one does wish the poor child wasn't under so much pressure.'

'Nonsense,' her husband said. 'Give them something to aim for. Best way to raise a child.'

'Do you have children, Mrs. Christie?' Mrs. Collyer asked.

'I have a daughter, yes,' Agatha replied. 'And you?'

Mrs. Collyer shook her head. 'No,' she said. 'No, we don't have children.'

'My work, y'see –' Mr. Collyer began, but then looked up at Mr. Finch as he appeared with sugar tongs, and a plate of patisserie.

'You did order these, didn't you?' the manager said, placing them in front of Mrs. Collyer.

'No,' Mr. Collyer began.

'Yes,' Agatha said, placing them squarely in front of his wife. 'We did.'

'I'm so sorry about the sugar tongs, Sir,' Mr. Finch said, placing a plate with tongs on it in front of him. 'It won't happen again.'

Mr. Collyer gave a harrumph of acknowledgement.

'You know, Mrs. Christie is a writer too, dear.' Mrs. Collyer took a pink macaroon from the plate and cut into it neatly with her dessert fork.

Mr. Collyer appeared not to hear. 'It's about getting the facts right,' he said. His gaze went to the tennis game again.

'He was very brave during the war,' Mrs. Collyer said. 'Dr. Adler. He was out in France, right by the frontlines. Something about camouflage. His wife told me all about it. Art and Science, working together, she said. She's a very nice woman, Mrs. Adler is. German, by origin. But settled in Britain long ago. Then after the war, one of his artist friends had come to live in Cornwall, so they retired here too. She obviously misses him terribly…' Her voice was soft. She glanced at her husband.

'So, you'll write that too?' Agatha asked him. 'About the war? People will be very interested.'

'The stabilization of sulphides is nothing to do with the war. I'm writing for chemists.' Mr. Collyer jabbed a finger towards the tennis courts. 'Now, that chap – he's a much better player than any so-called coach.'

On the courts, young Sophie Winters was engaged in a match with the smart, angular man.

'Kurt Farrar,' Mr. Collyer said. 'He's a family friend of the mother's, apparently. Stayed here before. If I was going to have a tennis lesson, I'd choose him before that Travers chap. In fact, I might just do that.' He drained his cup, got to his feet and went to watch the game.

The two women were left alone. Mrs. Collyer took a small éclair from the plate. 'My husband,' she said. 'He can be a bit abrupt. You must excuse him.'

'Of course,' Agatha said.

'The thing is –' her voice trembled slightly. 'He's rather anxious. This biography, it's been two years now – well, up until now it's all been very straightforward. Frau Adler has been ever so helpful, giving him the correspondence, showing him her husband's early work, that kind of thing. But it all changed just a couple of days ago. She's become very distant. Hostile, even. She seems not to trust Frederick any more. And neither of us knows why. Frau Adler has a friend, who stays here in fact, you'll have seen him – that gentlemen, Mr. Tyndall, he sits by the window at breakfast, tends to wear a hat? A nice man, an old friend of the family, he stays here every summer and spends a lot of time with Frau Adler. And he had a word with me yesterday, he was very anxious, something about Frederick having all Dr. Adler's papers. He said he'd gathered that Frau Adler

13

was losing patience, rather, with Frederick's work, and that she might withdraw her permission. We've yet to hear the truth of this. But of course, if that's the case, Frederick's life's work is completely ruined. He's always admired Dr. Adler. I think, to be honest, he envies him. Dr. Adler was unique in their field, and greatly admired. Other people have tried to write his biography, and I think Frederick's worried that his widow might change her allegiance to one of these other biographers.'

'Do you know her well?'

She nodded, smiled. 'Oh yes. I like her a lot. And her children, grown-up now, of course. A son and two daughters. And a charming grand-daughter too, she's five now, nearly six –'

'The same age as my daughter,' Agatha said.

'It's a lovely age.' Her eyes shone as she spoke. 'I would so love to have...' She stopped, gathered herself.

'It's not too late, surely –' Agatha said. The words came out before she could restrain them. 'I mean to say, you're still young.'

Mrs. Collyer met her eyes. 'Yes,' she said. 'I am still young. But my husband is adamant.'

'Nora!' the shout came from the tennis courts.

Mrs. Collyer jumped to her feet. 'Coming, dear.' She turned to Agatha. 'It's been lovely talking to you.' She gathered up her bag, crossed the room and descended the steps towards the tennis courts.

The sun had crept round and now shone a soft afternoon light across the palm court, flecking the edges of the swooping leaves.

On the tennis court, Mr. Farrar seemed to be demonstrating a move to Frederick, who was rather clumsily waving a tennis racquet in an attempt to imitate it.

Agatha drained her cup, got to her feet and went to her room.

*

"Captain Wingfield, do come and sit with us." Lady Bertram's voice rang out imperiously across the well-tended lawn. She stood, parasol in hand, at the top of the stone steps. He could see her two young daughters, laughing as they chased each other round the rhododendrons, under the steady gaze of their governess.

Captain Wingfield had noticed the governess the minute he'd first set eyes on her. There was something about her graceful step, her simple dress with its starched white collar, the seriousness of her expression.

"I think we're being called to tea," he said to her.

The young woman turned to him, and he saw a glimmer of amusement in her clear grey eyes. "Oh no," she said. "Not me. I have tea in the nursery. Lady Bertram has very strict rules..."

Agatha put down her pen. It was time to dress for dinner, she realized. It was still light, the pale blue evening light of early June. There would be cocktails on the terrace as the sun delayed its setting until well after the dinner gong had sounded.

Perhaps Archie's right. They'd discussed it last night, their last dinner together.

'What do you want to write a romance for?' he'd said. 'The murder stories are going so well.'

15

She'd tried to explain, about the Captain, the large country house, the Bertram family, 'Like people used to be, before the war –'

'Your readers will be so disappointed,' he'd said.

'My readers might enjoy the change,' she'd said. 'Certainly, I might enjoy the change.'

He'd looked out at the twilight across the bay. 'What do you know about romance?' he'd said.

Agatha laid her pearls down on the dressing table and stared at her reflection in the mirror.

Was it that beastly war? she asked herself. It had stood so much on its head. We were so young when we married, in haste, in the midst of uniforms and bag packing and the creeping, ever-present fear.

But we've been happy since. So lucky. A lovely home, a beautiful daughter, dear Rosalind, I must write to my sister and find out how they're all doing, how wonderful that I'll be seeing them all soon…

Her reflection stared back at her.

What do I know about romance, she wondered. Given that here I am, alone, on a holiday that was planned for two.

She fastened her pearls around her neck, patted her hair into place and left her room, closing the door softly behind her.

Chapter Three

Appearing in the dining room, she noticed two things: one, that she'd been seated with Mr. and Mrs. Collyer again. And, secondly, that Mr. Farrar seemed to be seated with them. She was aware of a conflict of feelings; firstly, a sense of dread, fearing another monotone and one-sided discussion about eminent chemists and cobalt stabilisation, and secondly, a flash of hope that this Mr. Farrar might be able to bring the conversation round to something more interesting.

The windows glowed with the last of the day's sunshine. The chandeliers sparkled. Once again Agatha was reminded of Archie's excellent choice in this hotel, even if he wasn't there to share it with her. She hesitated in the doorway. At a table by the window, sat the tennis party – Mrs. Blanche Winters, her daughter Sophie and their coach Sebastian Travers. The two women were in evening gowns, Mrs. Winters in pale blue silk with pearls at her neck, and the young Miss Winters in a rather severe grey, too old for her, thought Agatha, making her look pinched and angular, when a softer colour and more flowing style would have brought out her natural, fresh good looks.

In contrast, Mr. Travers was wearing a blazer and white trousers, as if determinedly trying to look like the tennis coach even at dinner. Agatha took in his upright posture and blond hair, and found herself thinking that perhaps Captain Wingfield might look rather like that.

Every time Mr. Travers said anything, Blanche flung her head back in merry laughter. Her daughter stared glumly out of the window.

Agatha approached her table, trying not to appear reluctant.

'Mrs. Christie.' Mr. Farrar was at her side. 'Allow me.'

A chair was pulled out for her. 'I do hope you have no objections to my joining you. Blanche was determined I stay with them, but I've had enough talk about forehand serves and landing positions. Also –' he lowered his voice so only she could hear – 'I thought you might need rescuing.'

Agatha flicked her long cream silk gown to one side and sat down. 'Thank you,' she said, hoping her tone conveyed her gratitude.

Mr. Collyer was staring into the bread basket. 'No butter?' he was saying. 'What do they think we are, continentals? I say –' a click of his fingers towards the waiting staff – 'what on earth is this?' He picked up the basket and waved it wildly. A piece of bread fell on to the floor.

Mr. Finch, the manager, was there at once. 'I'm sorry Sir, is there a problem?'

'There certainly is. No butter.'

'I'm terribly sorry, Sir. I'll get some at once.'

Mrs. Collyer had bent to the floor and retrieved the piece of bread. She handed it to Mr. Finch with an apologetic smile. He gave a brief, neat bow, then departed towards the kitchen.

'There was no need for that,' Mr. Collyer said to his wife. 'Acting like a maidservant.'

'I was only trying –'

'No need at all.' His face was grey as stone. The conversation seemed to be over.

Agatha was aware of Mr. Farrar at her side, tense, hardly breathing, it appeared. Now he smiled, breathed out. 'Well,' he said, 'has everyone had a lovely day?'

'Yes,' Mrs. Collyer said. 'Thank you.' But she seemed near to tears.

Their table was approached by another man. The solitary, military man, Agatha realized, who tended to eat alone. Mr. Tyndall, wasn't it? He had a kind face, she noticed, and a slightly shabby air, and gave a small bow as he greeted their table.

'Good evening,' he said. 'Mrs. Collyer. Mr. Collyer.' He offered his hand to Agatha, with a shy look in his blue eyes. 'I don't believe...'

Mr. Farrar was standing, his heels clicked together. 'Mrs. Christie, allow me to introduce Mr. Robin Tyndall.'

'Delighted,' Mr. Tyndall said, shaking her hand.

'And of course you know –' Kurt said.

'Of course,' he said, with another bow to Mrs. Collyer. 'I hope you're having a lovely stay here. The weather has been very much on our side.'

'How is Frau Adler?' Mrs. Collyer said.

'Well, thank you. I believe she's expecting you to call tomorrow. This matter of the papers –'

'It will all be sorted out,' Mr. Collyer said, brusquely. 'She must understand that I and I alone have the authority to write about her esteemed husband's life.'

There was a brief silence. 'I'm sure she does,' Mr. Tyndall said. Then, after another moment, 'Well, I bid you a good evening.'

He turned and went to his usual corner table, by the window overlooking the bay. The distant horizon was blurred to crimson with the ending of the day. The headland was darkening to twilight, pricked here and there by the yellow of a lamp.

'He always sits alone,' Mrs. Collyer said, her gaze following him. 'He's an admirable man. A great support to Frau Adler after her husband's death.'

'Another camoufleur,' Mr. Farrar said.

She nodded. 'They worked together during the War, Dr. Adler and Mr. Tyndall. Ernst worked on the chemistry of the paint, and Robin on the art of it, how to use design to hide from the enemy. They were deeply influential.'

'That will be an interesting chapter in your book,' Kurt Farrar said to Mr. Collyer.

'What?' He had torn a slice of bread into neat strips which now lay side by side on his plate.

'The *camoufleurs*. Fascinating bunch of chaps,' Kurt said.

'Dr. Adler was a chemist,' Mr. Collyer said, his tone abrupt. 'Lithopone, that's the stuff. Industrial pigment. That was his important work. Not messing about with plastic trees.'

'Oh.' Kurt stared at him, but there was no further conversation, and then the young dark-haired boy from the kitchen arrived with a dish of butter.

'About time,' Mr. Collyer said.

The boy was shy and rather thin, his skin sallow against his smart white jacket. He gave a mumbled apology and fled back to the kitchen.

'Do you know,' Kurt began conversationally, 'at the start of the war some of our chaps were on the front line wearing bright red uniforms? Until these clever men started working on shades of green and grey? That was the problem you see –' he produced a bottle of champagne from an ice bucket by his side and poured everyone a glass – 'previous wars, nineteenth century wars, we'd had the officer class in all their glory, all smartly turned out, riding on their prancing stallions. As if the whole thing was a glorious game. But this last war turned out not to be. Not a game at all.' His voice cracked. He picked up his glass and stared into it, twirling it in his fingers. 'There was no glory in those trenches. No honour. All there was, was mud. There we were, buried alive behind sandbags and barbed war. The colour of war had changed,' he said, almost to himself.

The table had fallen silent. The only noise was of Mr. Collyer scraping butter on to his bread.

The soup was served. Agatha was aware of Mrs. Collyer casting nervous glances at her husband. She wondered what things were like when it was just the two of them.

The quiet was broken by the floating laughter of Blanche from across the room. Then the piano started up, played by a large elderly lady in mauve satin.

'Drink up.' Kurt pointed at Agatha's champagne glass. 'There's another bottle here. Mr. Collyer?'

Mr. Collyer nodded, as Kurt refilled his glass.

'Mrs. Collyer?'

'She's had enough,' her husband said.

A glance flashed between Mr. Farrar and Mrs. Collyer, as she placed a hand over her glass. Her expression conveyed nothing.

'And how is your writing going, Mrs. Christie?' Mr. Farrar turned to her as the soup bowls were cleared.

'Perfectly well, thank you.'

'Detective stories, I gather.'

'I'm writing a romance,' she said, stiffly.

'Ah.' Mr. Farrar leaned back in his chair. 'Romance. The Happy Ever After of True Love. No wonder they call it fiction.'

Agatha studied him, but said nothing.

'Far better to stick with the facts, eh, Mr. Collyer.' He turned to his neighbour with a smile, with a trace of mockery too, Agatha thought. 'And a worthy subject. A biography,' Mr. Farrar said. 'We all need to read about exemplary men. An account of a person's life can tell so much. Why,' he turned back to Agatha, 'they'll be writing about you in due course.'

She stared at him. 'Me?'

'A famous author.'

'I'm not famous,' she said.

'But you will be. And then everyone will want to know about you.'

She put down her glass. 'Mr. Farrar – the idea horrifies me. People writing about me? Why on earth would they do that?'

'But you'll have devoted followers –'

'People can be followers of my work. That doesn't mean they should be followers of me.'

Kurt's eyes seemed to dance with amusement. She wondered whether he was ever serious.

'Oh, Kurt, why won't you join us?' Blanche's tinkling tone called across the room. 'Are we too frivolous for you?'

'Not at all, Blanche,' he replied. 'I just fancied a change.'

She laughed her girlish laugh, and Sebastian laughed too. Sophie fiddled her plait between her fingers.

Mr. Farrar's voice was low. 'It's a happy marriage, the Winters,' he said to Agatha. 'Contrary to appearances,' he added, as Blanche rested a delicate hand on Sebastian's arm. 'Her husband sends me with them each year to keep an eye on things, but he knows, deep down, he has no need. No need at all. She's devoted to her old man. A happy marriage – like your romance, Mrs. Christie? Except of course, your romance ends at the beginning, with the proposal. Unlike your crime stories, which begin at the ending. With the dead body.'

'Very clever,' Agatha said. She was trying to be annoyed with him, but in fact there was something engaging about him, his interest in her work, despite the surface sneer of superiority. There was also the sense that he wasn't telling the truth. Out of the corner of her eye she could see Sebastian clinking his glass with Blanche, and wondered what it was that Kurt wasn't telling her about the set up.

'So,' she said. 'The *camoufleurs*. These men who put their art at the service of the war. You seem to know a lot about them.'

He cast her a flicker of a smile, an acknowledgment.

'Hiding things,' she said. 'Saving lives.'

He nodded. But the smile had faded. 'Hiding things,' he repeated. He held her gaze and there was a haunted look in his eyes. She felt he was about to say more, but then, suddenly, he turned to Mr. Collyer and said, 'So, Adler's research was in dopant salts to stabilise zinc sulphide in relation to ultra violet light?'

Mr. Collyer lifted his head, turned to his neighbour and began to explain that it was more than mere zinc sulphide: 'A whole class of chemicals, lead hydroxide carbonate, zinc stearate, are extremely important in the preparation of plastics...'

Agatha half-listened. She watched Mrs. Collyer fiddle with the beads at her neck; she glanced from time to time at Mr. Tyndall, who barely touched his food and who in turn was casting fretful glances in the direction of the Collyers.

There were trolleys, new plates, dishes of potatoes placed on tables, beans, fresh-cooked steak.

Mr. Farrar seemed to have tired of the discussion of chemistry, and now poured some claret for Agatha.

'I don't really like wine,' Agatha said.

'At least taste it.'

'That's what people always say,' she said, with a smile.

'Your husband?'

'No,' she said. 'My husband understands me.'

'Ah,' Mr. Farrar said, and again there was that flash of mockery in his tone.

'What's this?' Mr. Collyer's voice was loud as he pointed at the plate placed before him.

'I'm sorry, Sir?' The pale young kitchen boy stood at his side, visibly trembling. 'It's your steak, Sir.'

'They know how I like my steak. What on earth is this?'

The boy seemed too frightened to reply.

'I like my steak rare. This is burnt to death.'

'I-I'll –'

Mr. Collyer was now on his feet, red-faced. His wife sat, deathly pale. Her eyes were closed, as if steeling herself, and Agatha felt touched by fear. Kurt too, seemed to feel it, and tensed next to her.

'How long have you worked here, boy?' Mr. Collyer now towered over the boy.

'Six months, Sir…'

'And have you not learnt, in all that time –' He jabbed a finger towards him. 'Have you not learnt what a rare steak ought to look like?'

The boy stepped back.

'Come here – I haven't finished –'

'I think you have, Sir.' The voice was calm and authoritative, and belonged to Mr. Finch. He seemed to have grown somehow, and now, as he faced Mr. Collyer, he looked quite tall. He rested a reassuring hand on the boy's shoulder. 'I gather there's a problem,' Finch said. 'Perhaps you'd like to tell me what the matter is.'

He stood, steady and very straight, his eyes locked with Mr. Collyer's.

'My steak is over-cooked,' Mr. Collyer said, but the words sounded oddly childish.

'I'm very sorry, Sir.' Finch didn't move. The word 'sorry' had acquired an edge of steel. Mr. Collyer seemed to shrink still further. 'We will see to it at once.' Finch bent to retrieve the plate, his hand still on the boy's shoulder. He faced Mr. Collyer again. 'I would be grateful, Sir, if in future you complained directly to me, rather than to my staff. The fault in no way rests with young Hughes here. He is doing his absolute best and does not deserve to be ill-treated. I will get you another steak right away.'

With that he steered the boy away from the table. The heavy kitchen door flapped shut behind them.

There was a silence. Mrs. Collyer opened her eyes, and breathed a short, tight breath. Mr. Collyer was still standing, but now sat down with a harrumph. The rest of the dining room settled again, conversations started up, the pianist began to play once more, Blanche's girlish laughter rang out as if nothing had happened. But Mr. Tyndall was staring directly at Mr. Collyer, with an expression of pure rage. As Agatha glanced at him, he lowered his head and returned to his untouched plate.

Mr. Collyer turned to his wife. 'Far too much for you,' he said, and reaching to her plate, spooned two potatoes back into the dish.

Agatha was aware that Mr. Farrar's fists were clenched at his side. 'He's worked here for years, Mr. Finch has,' he said. His voice was rather loud. 'Before and after the war, apparently. He was with the Royal Engineers. I bet his men always felt safe.'

The table began to eat, awkwardly, while Mr. Collyer waited for his steak. The elderly lady pianist played a Chopin nocturne. At last a new steak arrived, served by a red-faced middle-aged man wearing blue overalls; the kitchen porter, Agatha thought. Mr. Collyer helped himself to vegetables, and began to eat noisily. His wife was barely eating at all.

Mr. Farrar turned deliberately to Agatha. 'They're plundering that shipwreck.' His voice was a forced, conversational tone. 'Down in the village. Have you seen it?'

Agatha murmured that yes, she'd seen it that morning.

'The *Lady Leona*,' Mr. Farrar said. 'A fishing boat, floundered on those rocks some time ago. It's been rotting out at sea for a year and a day, which means that it's now legal for the villagers to strip it bare and see what they can find.'

'Gold,' Agatha said. 'That's what little May in reception said.'

He gave an easy laugh. 'Any sovereigns buried in the hold would have gone long ago,' he said.

'And ghosts,' Agatha added.

He looked suddenly grave. 'That's more likely,' he said. 'The sea claims its own. The villagers say there's a woman you can see,

27

sometimes. She stands on the cliff above the village, in the moonlight. There's a ruined cottage there. They say her husband was a sailor, drowned at sea, many years ago. They say she died of a broken heart, but there she is, waiting for him still.'

Agatha met his gaze. He appeared to be serious.

'Hauntings,' he said. 'Tales of the dead. Perhaps that's what you do when you write your murder mysteries.' His look was intense.

'My stories are more about the living than the dead,' she said.

He shook his head. 'What good is that?'

'Mr. Farrar – I make no great claims for what I do. In my work, order is restored, and life goes on.'

'Oh, Mrs. Christie. What can that tell us, about the human condition? There is no order. There is only grief, vengeance, suffering…'

'That's not what I do,' Agatha said.

'No?' His eyes flashed arid amusement.

'I wouldn't dream of describing the human condition.'

'Then your stories aren't true?'

'Mr. Farrar, they're stories.'

'But don't they have to be real?'

She considered this.

'I mean, our friend here –' he gestured to his neighbour – 'has to get his facts right, don't you, Mr. Collyer. Your biography has to be correct.'

'Of course.' Mr. Collyer smiled. His plate was empty, his good humour was recovered.

Mr. Farrar replenished Mr. Collyer's glass. 'Surely, whether a book is fact or fiction, it has to be true. And if you're writing about death, Mrs. Christie –'

'Mr. Farrar – my stories aren't about death.'

'Really?' Again, the look of dry amusement. 'In that case, what are they about? What is your detective doing?'

'My detective sees himself as protecting the innocent,' she said.

'From the guilty?'

She nodded.

He studied her. 'Oh, to live in your world, Mrs. Christie. Where that distinction is so clear.'

The table fell silent as Mr. Finch appeared and began to gather up the plates.

'I trust everything was in order, Sir.'

Mr. Collyer conceded that yes, it was, but he hoped it wouldn't happen again. Finch agreed, that indeed, it would not happen again. He announced the dessert was strawberry meringue. Mrs. Collyer said she wouldn't have any.

'But it's your favourite,' Mr. Finch said to her.

'I seem to have no appetite,' she said.

Mr. Collyer got to his feet. 'Too much cake at tea. Come along dear, I think we should retire.'

He went ahead of her towards the lobby. Finch moved away and began to serve the tennis party.

Mrs. Collyer turned to Mr. Farrar and Agatha, as if plucking up courage. 'Please forgive him,' she said. 'It's his work. All this business with Frau Adler, her threats to withdraw permission – it's making him very nervous.' She stood, winding her napkin between her fingers, then let it fall on to the table, before following her husband out of the room.

From his corner table, Mr. Tyndall watched them leave.

*

The strawberry meringue was exquisite. The pianist began to play something from a ballet, Tchaikovsky, perhaps. From the open windows the scent of sea air, a cooling breeze, the odd snatch of song from the seafront below.

'Kurt, do at least join us for dessert.' Blanche's voice was insistent, and at last Mr. Farrar excused himself, with Agatha's assurance that she was happy to eat alone. She watched him with the tennis party, wondering at the odd expression on Blanche's face whenever she turned to him, a kind of hovering concern. She wondered, once again, what he was hiding. She thought about his words on ghosts and grief, and guilt.

She refused offers of coffee, and after a while drifted away from the dining room and went to bed.

In her room she sat by the window, brushing out her hair. The moon shone across the bay. She thought about the sea claiming its own, the woman waiting for her husband who would never return.

*

She opened her eyes to bright sunlight, an awareness of deep sleep, a sense of possibility in her thoughts, Captain Wingfield in his scarlet jacket, the governess in her plain grey dress standing in the rose garden... and a ghost, yes, a woman waiting for her husband who would never return, she could even hear soft weeping.

It sounds so real, she thought, sitting up; and indeed, the weeping was still there, and now there were new sounds, raised voices, cries of distress, the shouts of men. She raced from her bed, went to the windows, pulled back the curtains.

She saw the sparkling blue of the sea, the white of the tennis courts. But it all seemed wrong, somehow. There were people, loud voices, an ambulance parked awkwardly across the grass, there were policemen, the revving of engines; and, above all the other noise, a choking, weeping sound, a woman crying out a man's name: 'Frederick'.

Chapter Four

The breakfast room was chilly, in spite of the morning sun. The tables were unset. There was not a member of staff to be seen. The guests stood in small awkward groups, staring out beyond the windows to the terrace.

The weeping had ceased.

Agatha had arrived in the room to hear, 'Mr. Collyer,' someone said. 'Shot dead...'

Outside there was fierce activity. On the tennis court there now stood a makeshift tent, white canvas blinding in the sunlight. Groups of people stood around, some in medical white, some in police blue.

'A bullet through the head,' someone said. 'Close range. That's what they're saying. Early this morning.'

The guests shifted, muttered, stared some more.

Agatha walked towards the French windows, through the drifting curtains, out into the sunlight.

'Mrs. Christie.' It was Robin Tyndall. He was standing on the terrace, watching the activity below. 'I trust you've heard the grim news.'

She nodded.

'Mr. Collyer,' he said. 'About six o'clock this morning, they think.'

'It was light,' she said. 'Someone would have seen it –'

He nodded. 'The staff rushed out – they heard the shot, they called the police.' He gestured with his head towards the commotion below them.

'But so early? What was Mr. Collyer doing on the tennis courts at such an hour?'

Mr. Tyndall hesitated. 'He rose early, I gather. His wife says he'd often go for a walk before breakfast.' He glanced at the police activity. 'And he'd said something about a tennis lesson too. He was even wearing tennis shoes. The strange thing is…' He faltered. 'Oh well,' he said. 'I'm sure the police know what they're doing.'

His tone was oddly abrupt. He turned to her, and said, as if to change the subject, 'I gather you have an interest in such matters.'

She shook her head.

'They say you write novels about such things?' he pursued.

There was a friendliness about his faded corduroy jacket, a comforting warmth in his blue eyes. She relented. 'I write novels, yes,' she said. She flicked a hand towards the tennis courts. 'It has nothing to do with this.'

He breathed, then said, 'All I was going to say was, that Mr. Collyer was found by Mr. Farrar.'

'That is odd, I agree.'

He seemed not to want to say any more. They stood in companionable silence. The scene below them was like a painting, with the bright blue of the sea, the low white walls, the groups of people poised.

Among the uniforms there were two other figures. One, a woman, in a slim dress of cherry red, full grey hair piled in a neat coil on her head. The other a man, thin-faced, black-haired, standing stooped and fretful by the tennis courts. He shifted, raised his eyes towards the terrace, lifted his arm towards Robin Tyndall in acknowledgement. The woman, too, gave a brief wave.

'That's Lillian Adler,' Robin Tyndall said. 'The widow of Dr. Ernst Adler. And that's his secretary, Mr. Fitzwilliam.'

'They're here very early,' Agatha said.

'The police must have sent for them,' Mr. Tyndall said.

'But –'

Mr. Tyndall turned to her. 'I fear…' he began. 'I fear it's this problem with the papers. The biography … Something was causing some friction between them all.' He raised an arm in greeting towards them, then turned back towards the French windows. 'Oh well,' he said. 'We'll soon find out, no doubt.' He yawned, stretched, as if to lighten the mood. 'I could do with some breakfast, couldn't you? Let's see if there's anyone in the kitchen who might fry a rasher of bacon. Ah – there's just the chap.'

As he spoke, Mr. Finch came into view, framed by the windows.

Agatha turned to join the guests, who were now clustered round the hotel manager, fretting, fussing, demanding. But before she went inside, she caught a glimpse of another figure, standing at a distance from the tennis courts – Kurt Farrar, in white shirt and loose white trousers, his hands clasped behind him. His gaze was fixed on the crime scene, glassy-eyed, shadowed with horror. Then he turned and disappeared towards the lower lawn.

The dining room had been transformed. An army of kitchen staff smoothed linen, laid tables, boiled eggs. The kitchen boy, young Hughes, was placing breakfast dishes on the hot-plates. There was a warm smell of bacon. The hungry, anxious guests had become chatty, smiling, even. Blanche Winters, seeing Agatha and Mr. Tyndall, indicated the two places at her table.

'Did you hear it?' she said, as Agatha sat down. 'The gunshot?' she went on. 'I heard it. I thought it was hunting to start with, until I remembered where I was. Did you hear it, Mr. Tyndall?'

Mr. Tyndall had to admit he didn't hear a thing. 'Still asleep, I was.' Agatha agreed she, too, had heard nothing.

'Six in the morning, they're saying, aren't they, Sebastian?'

The tennis coach was blond and groomed as ever, in spotless white. He smiled, nodded.

'Poor Sophie,' Mrs. Winters went on. 'You won't get on the courts for hours, now.'

Sophie pouted, shrugged.

'Heaven knows what it will do to her practice,' Mrs. Winters continued.

Sophie seemed not to be listening.

Then Agatha saw Mrs. Collyer, standing stock-still in the doorway, ashen-faced, her hair falling from its pins in loose strands. Mr. Finch appeared, led her to a corner table, poured her a cup of tea.

The boy Hughes had reappeared with a dish of poached eggs, and now Agatha saw him give a tiny wave to Sophie. Sophie blushed, giggled.

'Kurt,' Blanche was saying. 'Has anyone seen him?'

Mr. Tyndall said, no, he hadn't seen him. Agatha was wondering whether to mention that he was down by the courts, but Mrs. Winters was speaking again. 'This really is the last thing we need. My husband asked me to look after him, they're old friends, you see. He won't be pleased at all when he hears that I've brought poor Kurt into some kind of crime scene.'

Her tone was light, almost laughing, as if the whole thing was just a minor inconvenience, or an amusement laid on for the guests. But then her smile faded, and Agatha, looking in the same direction, saw Kurt appear in the doorway of the dining room. He had changed his clothes, and looked somehow clumsy, in a rough canvas jacket, wrongly buttoned, his hair untidy, a heavy frown across his features. Seeing Blanche and her party, he gave a cough, crossed to the table and sat unevenly into the spare chair.

'Did you hear?' He addressed the table. 'They've found the murder weapon,' he said. He gave a bark of laughter. 'It was just lying there, down by the tennis courts. A Weston Mark Six. A true soldier's weapon,' he said. 'Point blank range.' He held up his right hand as if holding a gun, flicked his finger against the imaginary trigger. 'Ka-pow,' he said, loudly. 'Your man falls to the ground. You drop the gun and run.' Another mirthless laugh.

Robin Tyndall had been quiet, finishing his plate of bacon and eggs. Now he looked up, uneasily.

'They're very excited, those policemen,' Kurt went on. 'And they're asking everyone, who found the body? But no one knows the answer. No one,' he repeated, as if it was a joke.

'Kurt – please,' Blanche said.

'What?' He gave a broad, unfocussed smile. 'I'm just catching you up with the news. And there's more,' he went on. 'Down there on the tennis courts, there's Frau Adler, widow of the old chemist, whose life our poor dead friend was trying to write about. It'll all be about that story, you mark my words.' He laughed, again.

'Kurt – you're not yourself.' Blanche placed a hand on his arm.

He shook her away. 'What, because I've had a drink? In my view, that makes me more myself than ever.' He beamed at the company, as if pleased with this.

Robin Tyndall got to his feet. 'Mr. Farrar,' he said. 'Come on. Let's find you a nice quiet cup of coffee somewhere.' He tucked his arm under Mr. Farrar's, levered him to his feet, and walked him out of the dining room.

Agatha noticed how Blanche gave an out-breath of relief.

She also noticed that Mr. Farrar was wearing white tennis shoes.

*

The morning wore on. Cars came and went. People came and went. The sun went in and rain clouds gathered. By lunchtime, the large band of policemen had dwindled to two or three, and the weather threatened drizzle. Outside, the one lonely local newsman had been joined by reporters from Truro and Exeter, burly men with tripods and flashlights.

Agatha escaped the hotel via the staff entrance and went for a walk.

The sky was grey, and a sharp wind buffeted the cliffs, but she breathed the fresh air with relief.

Word will get to London, she thought. She remembered the face of Mrs. Collyer, hollow-eyed with shock. She had disappeared to her room after breakfast and no one had seen her since.

Archie will worry, Agatha thought, as she tramped between the patches of gorse and heather. Perhaps I should get someone at the hotel to send word that everything's all right.

The air was crisp, the view sharp with beauty. Her spirits began to lift as she rounded the hill. The village lay before her. Once again she could see the skeletal curves of the shipwreck. The villagers were still busy, carrying its remains to the shore. It reminded her of something. A flash of memory; the pyramids at Giza before the war, a trail of workers carrying bricks against the undulating heat and sand. Even then, watching the ruins of the Giza Necropolis, the ancient pyramids rising up in the distance, even then she'd had a sense of the stories of the past buried deep within the scattered stones.

A snatch of music chimed with her thoughts. One of the women had stopped her work, and stood at the edge of the shore, singing. She was barefoot, in a loose, pale skirt and dark shirt.

'The tide flows in, the tide flows out, twice every day returning…'

The others stopped, listened.

'A sailor's wife at home must bide, he parted from poor me a bride, just as the tide was flowing…'

Some of the others began to hum along. Behind them rose up the jagged ribs of the broken ship, the remnants of men's livelihood, now become their coffin.

Clouds were hunched on the horizon.

'I stood here once in bridal white, but now I stand in mourning…'

Agatha listened to the sweet, clear voice. She thought about Mr. Farrar and his talk of grief. She thought about his bright white tennis shoes.

*

On the way back, picking her way between the gold and the purple, she looked up to see a young man pushing a bicycle along the track, further ahead. It took her a moment to recognize young Hughes, the kitchen boy. It took her another moment to see that the pretty girl strolling at his side, her face lit up with laughter, was Sophie Winters.

Chapter Five

The clouds had begun to lift. A thin ray of sunlight filtered across the hotel terrace.

Agatha had stumbled past the persistent journalists, and now found Mr. Finch standing in the red-carpeted hallway, as if expecting her.

'Ah, there you are, Madam,' he greeted her. 'Tea is being served in the Palm Court.' He looked somewhat reluctant, took a step closer, spoke in a low voice. 'I'm afraid to say that the Detective Inspector is with us. He wishes to question everyone. I tried to explain that it would be a terrible imposition on our guests, given that no one knows anything about these terrible events, but he said that the law must take its course. And I suppose that he is right in that regard. Detective Inspector Olds, he is, from the police station at Porthleven.' He sighed. 'At least he's local.'

He led the way towards the Palm Court. 'If you don't mind, Madam,' he went on, 'I've seated you with poor Mrs. Collyer. Her friend, Frau Adler is joining her, as the police wish to speak to her too. I have to say, Madam, my view is that it's a terrible way to treat people, pushing them around like that, and ladies too, it's not as if they're under the slightest suspicion. Any more than you are, Mrs. Christie.' He allowed himself a small smile, ushered her into the Palm Court and showed her to the table.

*

The table was still otherwise empty. Agatha was relieved to be left alone, for now at least.

The tennis party was already seated, and Mr. Farrar was with them. The unsteadiness had left him, and now his hair was combed, his shirt neatly buttoned. He was wearing dark brogues. He sat in a depressed silence. Sophie, however, was animated and smiling, even listening to her mother's chatter with polite respect.

The room was bright with sunlight and the fresh green of the palms. There was a clink of teacups, a low murmur of conversation, the tinkle of the piano, this time being played by a young man in a stiff white shirt and black jacket.

Then, in the doorway, there appeared the two women. One still in her cherry red dress. The other was wearing a pastel-flowered tea gown, which lent her an air of delicate beauty, despite the pallor of her face and her haunted, shadowed eyes.

'I gather we're joining you,' Frau Adler said.

Agatha smiled. 'My pleasure,' she said.

'In terrible circumstances, I fear.' Frau Adler had a very slight accent, an upright posture, and, Agatha noticed, elegant heeled shoes in black suede. She pulled out a chair for her friend, who sat down with demure weariness, then sat down herself.

'Frau Adler,' she said, offering her hand. She had an intense dark gaze. Her lips were painted a cherry red to match her dress.

Agatha introduced herself.

'I was here early this morning,' Frau Adler said. 'Early, early. And now they won't let me go home. I have dogs, waiting. They'll be howling. I only hope my neighbour has the sense to pop in with some titbits for them. The cats can fend for themselves, but the dogs, ach…'

Mrs. Collyer managed a thin smile. 'I'm sure they'll let you go soon, Lillian.'

'Perhaps they will, Nora. If not, I shall just get in my car and go home anyway. It's not as if they don't know where to find me. And if you had any sense, you'd come with me. You need friends around you, Nora dear, at such a terrible time. Terrible.'

Mrs. Collyer gave a tiny shake of her head.

'Stuck in a hotel, when such a ghastly thing has happened,' her friend went on, 'with that rabble of reporters outside like vultures. Ah, good, here comes tea. And with dear Olly too.'

Young Hughes the kitchen boy appeared with a large tray and now approached their table.

'Oliver dear, how lovely to see you,' she said.

The boy bowed his head, placed teapot and cups on the table.

'Some compensation for being kept prisoner here,' she went on, 'is that at least I get to see you.' Frau Adler patted his arm. 'I hope they're looking after you.'

'Oh, Mrs. Adler, they are. They are.' His voice burst with enthusiasm. 'I like it here very much. And Mr. Finch says one day he'll teach me to drive the car too.'

Frau Adler smiled. 'Good. You're a good boy.' She watched as he hurried back to the kitchens. 'And where is Mr. Tyndall, I wonder,' she said, her eyes searching the doorway. 'Well, never mind. I was rather hoping he'd join us. And as for our secretary, I think he's out with the Buick. He'd rather sit with the car than with me.' She gave a fond laugh. 'Oh dear, Nora, what are we to do? Such a mystery. Such a peculiar, ghastly thing to happen. Whoever would have wanted your husband to meet such a fate?'

Mrs. Collyer shook her head, blinked tearful eyes.

'One can only hope that this policeman will at least shed some light on the matter, given that he's gathered us all here.' Frau Adler reached for a cucumber sandwich, and cut it neatly in half. 'Ah, here at least is Mr. Tyndall.'

Robin Tyndall came to their table, bowed, and took the fourth seat. 'Ladies,' he said. He poured himself some tea. Agatha saw the unsteadiness of his hands.

'Oh, Robin, what are we to do?' Frau Adler gazed at him with dark eyes. Her dress was made of heavy silk, its frilled collar pinned with a large brooch of ornate silver. She turned to Agatha. 'When we first came to the village, my husband and I, we relied on Mr. Tyndall here to look after us. To show us how to behave.'

He smiled, briefly. 'Nonsense,' he began, but she went on.

'He has looked after us,' she said. 'Foreigners, you see. Incomers. And in these times too, my husband being so very German, me less so...' she laughed. 'You have been a friend to us, Robin,' she said. 'And then, when I lost my husband, two years, no, nearly two and half years ago now... Well, Mr. Tyndall has made sure I didn't sink into loneliness. Just me and the menagerie, it was indeed a danger. The children do what they can, but they have such busy lives...' She reached for another sandwich. 'And you were such a help to Frederick, too, when he came to me about my husband's work.'

'I tried,' Robin said. There was something rather tight-lipped in his reply.

She looked up, and a glance flashed between them.

'Yes,' she said. 'You tried.'

'These papers,' he began.

'Not now, Robin,' she said.

'You'll want them back,' he said, and his eyes rested on hers.

'All in good time,' she said.

It was Nora who spoke. 'You can have them all.' She spoke emphatically, wearily. 'They're no use to anyone now, are they?'

Robin reached across and patted her hand.

'But really,' Nora Collyer went on. 'All this fuss about Dr. Adler's papers, and Frederick ending up with them when you didn't really want to part with them, and now he's dead, and it doesn't matter does it? It doesn't matter what he was going to say about your husband and whether it was right or wrong?' Her eyes flashed with rage, with grief. Her voice cracked with tearfulness.

There was a brief silence. Around them the Palm Court settled back to its quiet hum of tea and conversation.

Lillian Adler leaned across to Mrs. Collyer. 'My dear Nora,' she began. 'I'm so sorry. As you say, it really doesn't matter now. There are far more important things to worry about than a few letters. However...' She glanced at Robin, then turned to Mrs. Collyer again. 'However, it would be nice to have them back sooner rather

44

than later. Given that, as you say, it doesn't matter now. We don't want them getting all mixed up in the police investigation, do we?'

Nora Collyer sniffed, patted her pretty hair. She nodded. 'I'll try and find them for you,' she said.

'Good,' Frau Adler said. 'I do think that would be best.'

She then turned to Agatha. 'Art and Science, you see,' she said. 'My husband was a linchpin between the two. Is that the right expression, Robin?'

'Well…' his tone was hesitant. 'If you mean –'

'I mean, the war,' she interrupted. 'These men, Mr. Tyndall knows too, their work was beyond compare. The marriage of chemistry know-how and artistic genius – and bravery too… Oh, the lives they saved. I know we were German by origin, but our home is here, our children are British … I am proud of what my husband did.' She stopped, breathless.

'Camouflage,' Mr. Tyndall said, as in explanation. 'Dr. Adler worked on types of paint that would survive a war environment. Pigment, you see, that would reflect light rather than absorb it, keep the enemy guessing.'

'Lithopone.' The voice was loud, and Agatha realized that Kurt Farrar was crossing the room towards them. 'That's what you're all on about, isn't it?'

'Mr. Farrar.' Mr. Tyndall got to his feet. 'Frau Adler, allow me to introduce Mr. Kurt Farrar. Another guest here…' He glanced at Mr. Farrar, then fell silent.

Kurt Farrar gave a deep bow.

Lillian Adler acknowledged him with a turn of her head, but her face was set, and her eyes narrowed as he shook her hand.

'Mr. Farrar also knows something of the camoufleurs, don't you?' Mr. Tyndall's voice was clipped.

'I served in the Somme,' Mr. Farrar said. 'I was aware of their work. Magical stuff. All those battleships undetected. All those tanks, creeping up to enemy lines –' He threw Frau Adler a charming smile.

'Hardly tanks, Mr. Farrar,' Mr. Tyndall said.

'Ahead of the game, we British,' Mr. Farrar went on, as if he hadn't heard. 'Sending our boys into battle but keeping them hidden. Camouflage, see? You either obscure things, or you disguise them. A metaphor for life, wouldn't you say, Mrs. Christie?' Again, a mirthless laugh. He pulled up a chair, as if they'd invited him to join them. 'And then it turns out they were here, the artists, down the road here, beavering away, perfecting their techniques. Pointillism, Cubism, anything to create a false version of the truth.'

'Down the road?' Agatha asked.

'Oh yes. Towards the village there. Ince Hall. Empty now, of course. A mere ruin. But at the start of the war, a hive of activity. All those chaps. A power house of creativity, wasn't it, Mr. Tyndall?' He turned to Robin Tyndall, bright-eyed, expecting affirmation.

Mr. Tyndall glanced at Lillian, then at Agatha. 'Dr. Adler was enlisted to help,' he said, as if in explanation. 'His expertise in pigment was invaluable.'

'It should have all gone in the book,' Kurt said. He looked across at Mrs. Collyer, as if he'd only just noticed her. 'Too late now, I suppose.' The colour had drained from his face, and his voice quietened. 'Too late,' he repeated, with an air of melancholy. Agatha once again wondered at the theatricality of his utterances.

Mrs. Collyer had lowered her gaze, and was staring, unseeing, at the table, the cake stand with its tiers of untouched pastries. Lillian lent across and laid her right hand over Mrs. Collyer's left.

The piano playing stopped, mid-phrase. The conversation around them hushed. In the doorway, a uniformed police officer had appeared, and now uttered a few words to Mr. Finch, who was also standing by the door. Finch gave a brief nod, then turned to the room.

'Ladies, Gentlemen. My apologies for the interruption. But if you have all finished your tea, the Detective Inspector would like everyone to assemble in the lounge.'

There were murmurs of acquiescence, some of complaint. Hats were taken up, bags gathered, and the party trooped through the door, down the red carpeted corridor, to the hotel lounge.

Chapter Six

The lounge was huge and high ceilinged, all red and gold, with sufficient settees and chairs to seat the assembled party. Mrs. Winters took one of the generous sofas, with Sophie on one side and Sebastian on the other. Frau Adler took one of the smaller ones, and patted the seat next to her for Nora Collyer. Robin Tyndall tucked himself into a corner, and Agatha took a small seat next to the window. The velvet drapes framed the square of garden in the late afternoon sunlight, the pink-sparkled ribbon of sea beyond.

Mr. Finch had assembled the staff, all of whom stood in a neat, starched line by his side. Young Oliver Hughes had the place next to him. Agatha noticed the boy catch the eye of Sophie Winters and a small smile passed between them.

In the middle of the room sat the Detective Inspector and another official looking man. Neither were in uniform. They both got to their feet. There was an air of calm, as the older man began to speak.

'Ladies, Gentlemen, thank you for your time this afternoon. I'd like to introduce myself. My name is Detective Inspector Reginald Olds, and this is Detective Sergeant Brierley. We are members of the Cornwall Constabulary, and we've been brought in today because of the very unfortunate events of this morning.' He glanced towards Mrs. Collyer. She sat, eyes lowered, her hands in her lap.

'I'll try not to detain you for long,' he went on. 'I'd like to furnish you with the facts. So, this is what we know. At something before six this morning, Mr. Collyer rose and said he was going to play tennis. Mrs. Collyer was perfectly accepting of this, as it gets light very early at the moment. Her husband directed himself to the tennis courts. Now, we know two things. One, is that he had been invited for that game of tennis by Mr. Kurt Farrar. So Mrs. Collyer tells us.' He looked around the room, but Mr. Farrar was nowhere to be seen. Agatha noticed Mrs. Winters flicking nervous glances towards the door. Mr. Farrar must have slipped away when they were all trooping into the lounge, she thought.

The detective was speaking again. 'The second thing we know, is that that game never took place. Before any balls were struck, Mr. Collyer was dead, on the court out there. The single shot was heard by the staff, who then ran out to the court, saw what had happened, and sent for my team.' He paused, surveyed the room, then continued. 'The third point is that the weapon we assume to be the murder weapon, a revolver, was left at the scene of the crime and is being examined by our forensic team. Now, there are two possibilities. One, is that poor Mr. Collyer's killer had arrived here in secret, drawn his murder weapon, carried out his evil deed and then fled. The alternative –' His gaze settled on the company in front of him – 'is that no one fled at all. That the culprit shot his victim, dropped the pistol, and then calmly returned to the hotel. In which case, he or she is amongst you still.'

He paused and took a sip from the glass of water by his side. 'Now, the staff here have been exceedingly helpful to me and my boys. So, this is what we know. The only people up and about at the time of the killing were the staff, and Mr. Kurt Farrar.' He looked towards Mrs. Winters, to the empty chair at her side. He went on, 'Mr. Collyer had no enemies. He had lived a quiet and uneventful life as a chemist, and had recently embarked, in his retirement, on this work of biography, the subject of which was Dr. Adler, who lived in the village here, with you, Frau Adler, his wife.'

Lillian Adler tilted her head in acknowledgement.

'Mr. and Mrs. Collyer had taken to staying here for some weeks of each year to pursue his researches. This was your third visit, I believe, Mrs. Collyer?'

Mrs. Collyer looked up. She nodded. Even in her state of shock, she looked poised and softly elegant.

'The family of Dr. Adler had become friends, had they not?'

Again, a small nod from Mrs. Collyer.

'So even there,' the policeman went on, 'there is nothing to suggest the kind of enmity that would result in such a grievously harmful act. Dr. Adler was an eminent man in his field, a specialist in pigment. Despite his origins, he was very much an Englishman, and he'd helped our boys with the war effort in the application of camouflage in the field. He had settled in this area with his wife and lived a quiet life until his death, two years ago, at the age of eighty-two.' Detective Inspector Olds sighed. 'Well, that is all that there is to be said. We will continue our investigations, of course –'

He was interrupted by a loud swish as the lounge door swung open and Kurt Farrar strode into the room. 'Ah!' he said. 'All here, I see.' He scanned the gathering with a mirthless smile. 'And there's even a chair for me. How kind.' He flung himself into the chair at Mrs. Winter's side, and then sat back, as if waiting for a show to start. 'Well, here I am.'

The room seemed to shift around him, Agatha noticed. In particular, Blanche's pale bejewelled fingers were signalling to him, as she mouthed something, some kind of warning, it seemed. And Mr. Tyndall, too, sat upright and apprehensive, his hands smoothing his trousers.

Kurt gave his empty smile again. 'Well – don't let me interrupt,' he said.

Blanche's finger went to her lips, but he seemed not to see this, and continued to speak. 'Are we hearing the story of the tragic untimely death of Mr. Collyer? Do go on.'

Detective Inspector Olds stood tall and calm. He fixed Kurt with a steady gaze. 'I'm afraid I've said all there is to say,' he said. 'So far,' he added.

'Have you told them about the tennis shoes?' Kurt said to him. 'That I was seen, that morning, wearing tennis shoes?'

The Detective showed a faint twitch of annoyance. Kurt went on, 'I'd invited the deceased to a game of tennis. Did you tell them that? Pre-breakfast tennis.' He laughed. 'But it never happened. I came down a bit late, typical I'm afraid. No sign of him. Went to look for him inside. Heard the shot. Came out. There he was. Poor b – poor soul,' he corrected himself.

Blanche's fingers fluttered their distress.

The policeman still had his gaze fixed on him, but said nothing.

'Gunshot, you see.' Kurt surveyed the room. 'It has a particular sound.' He paused, as if for effect. 'Close range. The blood … and the smell … warm blood. Fresh … Never forget it … At that range, y'see … blasted apart … scarlet, the blood … before it goes crimson …'

Blanche's signalling had become frantic waving, but Kurt didn't look at her.

The policeman now spoke. 'So you agree, Mr. Farrar, that you were first on the scene?'

Kurt Farrar raised his head, as if seeing Inspector Olds for the first time. His voice was thin. 'So it seems.'

The Inspector spoke again. 'From what we can gather from the staff, you were there when they ran outside, having heard the gunshot. They found you, right in the middle of the tennis court.'

Kurt gave a brief nod. 'That's quite likely,' he said. 'I was due to give the poor man a tennis lesson.'

Blanche was now gesturing to Mr. Tyndall, who cleared his throat. 'I think that's quite enough for now,' he said.

'On the contrary –' Kurt's voice was loud, as he threw Blanche an empty grin. 'Our poor policeman here has hardly started. But he's asking the wrong questions. The biography,' Kurt said. 'That's the clue. Secrets to be revealed.'

Mr. Tyndall flashed a glance at Frau Adler.

'Oh, we all have secrets,' Kurt went on. 'Why, look at this room. Every single one of us is hiding something. It's the human condition. Detective Inspector, if you were to ask each person here to confess to a secret, even just one each – you'd have days and days of work to keep your chaps busy.' He laughed, loudly.

Blanche signalled again to Mr. Tyndall, who got to his feet. 'I think this interview is over now,' he said. 'Unless there is anything further we can help you with, Inspector?'

The Detective Inspector looked at Kurt Farrar, and then seemed to reach a decision. 'Nothing at this stage, thank you, Sir. Oh, just one other thing – until we find out the perpetrator of this terrible deed, you are all … well, not to put too fine a point on it, you are all …'

Kurt gave his loud, empty laugh. 'Suspects? Is that the word you're after, Inspector?'

'I simply meant, Sir, that I'd prefer it if all the people who were guests in this hotel at the time of the crime, if they could all continue to stay here.'

'Under house arrest,' Kurt said, to a loud 'Shhh' from Blanche.

The Detective looked at him levelly. 'All I meant, Sir, was, that a sudden flight might be seen as suspicious. And now we'll bid you a good evening.'

He crossed to the door, followed by his Sergeant, who scuttled out behind him with a breath of relief.

Mr. Tyndall was at Mrs. Collyer's side. He offered her his arm. 'Allow me, Madam.'

She looked up, surprise and relief on her face. She rose to her feet and allowed him to lead her from the room. The others got to their feet.

Kurt was still spread across his chair. 'Oh,' he said, amused. 'Is that it, then?'

Blanche had taken the chair next to him. 'You promised.' Her voice was low, almost a whisper. 'No more drinking.'

'Half a glass of decent brandy,' he said. 'Medicinal, when a man's had a shock.'

'No more,' she said. 'You promised my husband, no more drink …'

'Promises, Madam. Not worth the paper they're written on …'

She shook her head, then looked around for Sophie, who had stayed where she was, her eyes on the staff.

Mr. Finch was tidying the room, rearranging the chairs. In the corner, Frau Adler was still seated, with young Oliver Hughes at her side. They appeared to be deep in conversation, her hand on his arm in a gesture of affection.

Blanche now took Sophie by the hand and they headed for the door. A glance passed between Sophie and Oliver as mother and daughter left the room.

Frau Adler patted the boy's arm, got to her feet. The boy went to Finch and began to help him load a tray with cups.

In the doorway there stood a man. He was angular, expressionless, with smooth black hair and a pale cashmere jumper, which sat oddly against his stiff formality. 'Frau Adler,' he said. 'I've brought the car round to the front.'

'Oh, Quentin, dear, how very thoughtful of you.'

As she walked towards him, the man caught sight of Kurt Farrar. The look between them cut through the room. Kurt sat, frozen, his gaze locked with that of the other man. The other man's face softened with a flicker of recognition. Then he turned, gave a small bow, and left the room, with Frau Adler at his side.

Agatha too, got to her feet, and headed for the door. When she looked back, Kurt Farrar was still sitting, his gaze fixed on the doorway.

Chapter Seven

There was a silence about the hotel, as afternoon faded into evening. Agatha ordered a cold supper, which she ate in her room. It was as if after the shock of the events, every inhabitant of the hotel had hidden away. The sky clouded over with the last of the day, and the windows rattled with a sharp sea breeze.

After her supper, Agatha ventured downstairs again. The lounge was deserted. The dining room too was deathly quiet, apart from the occasional gust of wind across the terrace outside. She was aware of music, distant notes floating across the hushed space. She followed its direction and came out into the Palm Court. The tables were bare, the chairs empty. But from the piano came a Chopin prelude. And at the piano sat Nora Collyer.

The melancholy notes filled the space, which had a sombre light from the stormy sunset. After a few moments, the piece came to an end, the last notes settling sweetly. Then Nora looked up and saw Agatha standing there.

'He didn't mention the papers.' The voice was soft, the words direct.

Agatha wondered what to say.

'The Inspector,' Mrs. Collyer went on. 'He must have known that Frau Adler had requested that my husband return the papers.'

'Perhaps he didn't want to embarrass you,' Agatha said. 'Or her.'

'Perhaps.' Nora hesitated. 'Though it's no embarrassment to me. I always felt that she would be within her rights not to let my husband intrude on her privacy like that. She knows that's how I feel. I wasn't at all surprised when we heard that there might be a problem.'

'How did you find out?' Agatha took a few steps towards the piano.

'Mr. Tyndall mentioned it to us. Only a couple of days ago, in fact. He said he'd heard that Frau Adler was becoming nervous about some of the papers, the more recent correspondence, and things from the war ... She'd asked for them back. It made my husband rather angry.'

'And did he return them?'

She shook her head. 'Mr. Tyndall was telling him he had to. And then yesterday, they had quite an argument, I'm afraid to say. Well, you saw what my husband was like. He could be rather – abrupt, shall we say, when roused. Mr. Tyndall surprised us in the corridor out there, after my husband's afternoon stroll. It was as if he'd been lying in wait for our return. Rather out of character too, I thought at the time. Mr. Tyndall has always been a gentleman. But really, he was so very definite about the need to have the papers back, and voices were raised. It really was rather odd. "Dire consequences," that was the phrase that Mr. Tyndall used. "Dire consequences".'

Agatha considered this. Mrs. Collyer went on, 'I'm sure Frederick intended to return them, but he's very stubborn, my husband. Was,' she added, as if, once again, struck by the finality of his death. Her eyes welled with tears. She bowed her head, sitting there with her hands in her lap.

'He was still my husband,' she said. 'A wife … a wife has to love her husband, hasn't she? That's what my mother said …'

Agatha drew up a chair and sat down next to the piano stool.

'They're all still up there, the papers,' Nora went on, 'a big box of them. I suppose I should tell that policeman. I was going to give them back to Lillian, but then this happened, and then I didn't know what to say, in case they're evidence or something. Do you think I should tell that nice Detective?'

In her mind, Agatha saw Frau Adler's insistence about the papers again, the 'not wanting to bother the police with all that …' She turned to Mrs. Collyer. 'I think, perhaps, you should.'

Mrs. Collyer sniffed, nodded.

'You play very well,' Agatha said.

Nora touched the piano keys with her fine fingers. 'I learned as a child. But it's been a while …' she murmured.

'You must practice a lot,' Agatha said.

Nora shook her head. 'No, no. My husband doesn't … didn't … he didn't like it. I play when I visit my brother Peter and his family, they have a lovely instrument there, I can spend hours on it. I do it to amuse the children too …' She gave a brief, luminous smile. 'My brother's old friend James teases me, he makes me sing as well. He says I have the voice of an angel …' The smile died. 'But my husband has to work you see, he doesn't like noise in the house, he needs to concentrate … Needed to concentrate,' she corrected herself. '"No extraneous noise", he used to say.' She shook her head, dabbed at her eyes. After a moment, she said, 'You have a husband, don't you?'

'Yes.' Agatha wondered what she meant.

'He was here, wasn't he. And then he went away.' Mrs. Collyer was facing her directly.

'Yes,' Agatha said. 'He had to go back to work.'

'You seem to be managing without him. But it's not final, is it,' Mrs. Collyer went on, as if it had just occurred to her. 'I mean, your husband, he'll be back in your home, thinking about you, and you'll be thinking about him, and he's probably worrying about you, if word about all these terrible events reaches him. Whereas me ...' She raised tearful eyes to Agatha. 'There's no one now. No one to worry about me. Ever again. Well ...' She produced a white linen handkerchief, and wiped away her tears. 'I shall just have to get on without him. I don't know how. Mother will say I've only got myself to blame.' She got to her feet and turned towards the door. The dainty click of her shoes against the parquet floor faded into silence.

My husband, Agatha thought. Worrying about me. It was an odd thought. In her mind, a picture of the golf club at Sunningdale. Her husband, standing on the green in the summer evening light, pausing, mid-swing, to worry about his wife.

Of course he'll worry, she thought. Particularly if an account of these events reaches the London papers. I really must let him know I'm all right, she thought. Yes, she thought. Tomorrow. I'll pop to the post office and send a telegram. Dear Archie, she thought, that will put his mind at rest.

*

Overnight, the wind had dropped. The day dawned grey and still, casting a melancholy silence over the hotel. After breakfast, taken alone in the muted dining room, Agatha set out to the village post office.

Across the bay, the sun tried to break through the scudding clouds. The rough path descended to the village. Agatha saw, once again, the crooked form of the recovered ship, its black lines softened by the low mist. The Post Office sat at the centre of the village street, a square of creamy white amidst the blue-grey stone.

That's the colour, she thought. That's what I need for my story, for the stone walls of the rose garden, where Captain Wingfield waits for Miss Hobbes the governess to pass by. He will watch her as she approaches, his heart beating in anticipation. She will walk towards him, graceful in her simple dress, and he will compose in his mind the words he wants to say to her ...

Agatha felt a quickening pleasure at the thought of her work waiting for her, her notebook on the mahogany table by the window in her room. She pushed at the door, which rang loudly with bell chimes.

The Post Office seemed full of people, and they all, as one, turned to stare. She was aware of hats, ladies, fishing boots, overalls, beards. Then the murmur of conversation started up again.

In her mind, as she waited, she composed the few words of her telegram. 'Unfortunate events at hotel. Stop. All well. Stop. Will come back as planned. Stop.'

'I'll see you on Sunday,' Archie had said on the station platform, holding her in his arms. 'I'll be counting the days,' he'd said, holding her tight. Captain Wingfield will take Miss Hobbes in his arms and hold her tight. 'I've been counting the days,' he'll say to her. 'We were meant to be.'

Agatha realised that all eyes were upon her, and that the post mistress, a fierce-looking, starch-collared woman, was waiting. She went to the counter and dictated her telegram, aware too that various hats, beards and overalls were listening to her every word.

We were meant to be. She almost added it to the telegram. 'We were meant to be. Stop.' That would have given the audience of villagers something to wonder at. Instead, she thanked the post mistress, paid and left, sweeping out of the door to the ring of the bell.

The mist had lifted. The little high street dazzled in sunlight. She blinked in the brightness, and almost collided with Detective Inspector Olds.

'Mrs. Christie –' He raised his hat.

'I'm sorry –'

'Quite all right, Madam.' He faced her, standing in the village street.

'I trust I'm allowed to come this far,' she said.

He gave a dry smile. 'I didn't mean you, Madam,' he said. 'I was just taking precautions regarding certain other guests.' His lined face crinkled into a smile. 'Come to see our archaeology have you?' He waved a hand towards the ship reclamation.

'Well …' she began.

'It is quite a tale,' he said. 'If you like a good yarn.'

'I – er –'

'Some will say they scuppered it on purpose all those years ago, lured it on to the rocks to filch the treasure. Some will tell you a more ordinary tale, of high seas and stormy winds and the everyday tragedy of sailors drowned at sea.' He was turned towards the beach, his eyes following the to-ing and fro-ing of the villagers.

'And you, Inspector Olds?'

He turned back towards her, and now there was a darker, sorrowed look about him.

'I knew them,' he said. 'The three drowned men. The skipper best of all.' His gaze turned back towards the beach. 'Friends, you see. Me and Mikey. Went to Mitching School together. We'd take our bikes, hide out at Abey's Bay. We'd fish, sail … that boy could make a seaworthy vessel out of a plank of wood and half an old bed-sheet …' His eyes were clouded as he faced her again.

'And which version do you believe? About the shipwreck?' She spoke gently.

There was a sudden fire in his expression. 'Not a single one of these villagers would lure a sailor to his death. Not one. We are of the sea, we Cornishmen. We have saltwater in our veins. We look out there and gaze upon the waves, and know that what we see is both our friend and our foe. And knowing that, we love it still. No …' He shook his head. 'The Lady Leona was just steering the course that the fates had dictated for her. As we all must do.' He gave a small smile. 'Well, Mrs. Christie, I must get to work. I'm headed up to the big house to find out a bit more about poor Mr. Collyer.'

'To see Frau Adler?'

'I hope so. Not that she's invited me. They've kept themselves quiet, they have.' He began to walk up the hill. 'People called them the Germans.'

'She seems to know the kitchen boy.'

'Young Hughes. Yes. We think warmly of her for that in any case.'

'What happened?'

Again, a shadow of sadness. 'The war carried off a good few of our men. And Hughes, the boy's pa, was one of them. And then the mother died, the flu she got, after the war. Young Olly was orphaned. And the Germans took him in. Raised him as their own. He's doing very well now.' They fell into step together, on the road that led away from the village. After a moment, he said, 'This book, that the deceased was writing, about Dr. Adler …'

She waited. He went on, 'It seems, shall we say, controversial. I don't know how much you know about the goings on here, but Dr. Adler, it is said, had connections with some scientists in Russia. And Mr. Collyer seemed to have got hold of some papers that were something to do with all that, and Dr. Adler's wife had just recently asked for them back.' He walked a few more steps, then went on,

'These Soviets, see,' he said. 'We fight a war on one front, and then another one appears. Not that I want to go pointing any fingers. But the funny thing is, my friend Bosun Walker, who's keeping an eye on things here, with this ship being stripped of all its rotten cargo, well, the Bosun said he'd seen odd goings-on on the beach here, one night last week. He said he saw a man and a woman on the beach here, and they seemed to be waiting, as if for a boat to come in. And he reckoned that the woman of the couple was Frau Adler. He said he hung about a bit, but there was no sign of any vessel, and after a while he left them to it.' He paused in his walking. 'Still, can't start reading too much into things like that. They may be Bolsheviks, but in this country we're all innocent till proved guilty, like it or not. So, that's why I'm headed up to the House now, to have a bit of a chat with them. Just a friendly chat, see. The important thing, in my line of work, is the facts. That's what I'm after. The facts.'

They walked on. It had become a bright, summery day. The sea was now a glassy blue.

'Bolshies,' Inspector Olds was saying. 'You can't be too careful. We didn't fight a war just to have that lot creeping around amongst us, eh? My motor car's just here. Can I offer you a lift? It's no trouble.'

Agatha smiled, shook her head, insisted she'd enjoy the walk back to the hotel. He started his car, jumped in, and with a loud phut-phut of the engine, drove away up the hill.

She walked along the coastal track, reflecting on their conversation. She wondered whether she should have mentioned what Mrs. Collyer had told her, about the disputed papers being in her hotel room. The image came to her of the delicate, newly-widowed Nora. I couldn't do that to her, she thought. The police must find that for themselves.

Her stout shoes crunched the gorse underfoot. The wind had got up again, ruffling the long grass around her.

To lose one's husband, she thought. Not to have him waiting for you, not to have those arms around you, those sweet words whispered. So many of us suffered such a loss, she thought. So many soldiers, sailors, air-men, didn't come back. But at least, with war, there's a reason. Whereas a dull, portly man, shot dead on a tennis court –

'I say! They've let you out, then?'

The voice came from behind her, and she turned to see Mr. Farrar striding up the track towards her. 'I suppose you don't look like a murder suspect, Mrs. Christie. Unlike yours truly here. I had to give them the slip just to get a breath of air. Enjoying the sea breeze, eh?'

She agreed that, yes, it was pleasant to be out.

'Even dear Blanche agreed I should come out,' he said. 'She said I'd only drink again if not. Probably glad to get rid of me for a bit. So –' he fell into step beside her. 'What do you make of all these goings-on back at the ranch?'

Agatha murmured something about the police investigation, about how she was sure they'd uncover the truth in due course.

'How very trusting of you, Mrs. Christie.' The smile was edging towards its characteristic sneer. She chose to ignore it.

'Blanche is right, of course,' he went on. 'She always is. She knows I'm no good at boredom. Pathologically allergic to it, in fact. *L'ennui*, you see.' His tone was conversational as he walked by her side. 'Not just boredom. It's the feeling of the age, in my view. Lethargy, despair … le cafard, we called it, in France.'

He walked slowly, dragging his feet. The wind buffeted them, flicking the distant sea.

'And did boredom drag you down to Cornwall, then?' she asked him.

He flashed her a glance. 'Boredom,' he agreed. 'And relatives.'

They reached a fork in the path. He pulled out his pocket watch with a theatrical gesture. 'We still have time,' he said. 'Oodles of time.'

'For what?'

'For visiting the old ruined manor. The hide-out of the war-time artists. That was my plan for today. I've always meant to see it.' He flashed her a look. 'You could come too, if you like.'

'Come where?'

'Ince Hall, it's called. It's an old manor house, over in the woods there. Built by Catholics, apparently, about three centuries ago. It's a ruin now. It's where all the artists gathered at the start of the war.'

'The *camoufleurs*?' she asked.

He nodded. 'The *camoufleurs*.' He reached for her hand. 'Come with me, Mrs. Christie. It's either that or a cold ham lunch back at the hotel with all the other suspects.'

She smiled in acquiescence, fell into step at his side.

They set off along the path that led away from the coast, across a rough field. The sun began to break through the clouds, and after a while Agatha began to feel rather heated.

'Telegram, was it?' His voice interrupted her thoughts.

'I beg your pardon?'

'At the post office. Telling your poor husband that we're all under house arrest now.'

She stopped and faced him. 'Yes,' she said. 'Actually. It seemed only sensible.'

'Of course.' A nod of his head in concession. He set off along the path again. 'It must be nice to be needed,' he said, after a moment. 'To have someone who cares.'

'Yes,' she said. 'It is.'

'Soldier, was he?'

'Airman,' she said.

The words stopped him. He turned to her, his eyes alight with interest. 'Air man? Which squadron?'

'Number Three Squadron,' she said. 'Royal Flying Corps.' She wondered which version of Mr. Farrar she preferred, this taut, burning interest, or the phony-seeming lassitude of earlier on.

He began to walk again, now striding, energetic, his hands in his pockets. There were trees either side of them, and the path had narrowed. 'I know the turning is here somewhere, I stumbled upon it the other night – hah –' he exclaimed, as they rounded a corner, all gnarled oaks and brambles. 'Here, look.' He pointed.

In front of them was an arch in golden stone, half-smothered with ivy. A paved path led away from it. Nestling beyond she could see a mansion of some kind, a sprawling, gold-stone building with tall gracious windows and wide lawns.

'Ince Hall. Come on.' Boyish now, he loped ahead of her. As she followed, she realized that the house was a ruin, the windows cracked, the grand front door hanging at an angle, the curved lawns overgrown with weeds.

Kurt had run up to the front door and now stood with his hand placed flat against the peeling green paint. 'Here,' he said. 'Who'd have thought?'

Breathless, she caught up with him.

'During the war,' he said. 'They were stationed here.'

'Who?'

He had pushed the door open, and now ventured into the hall. She followed.

It was a tall, dingy space. The parquet of the floor was twisted with damp, strewn with leaves. The walls showed dusty squares where paintings had hung. High above, a beam of sunlight cut through the stale air.

'"I shall suffer nought so dreadful as an ignoble death".' Kurt spoke softly. He seemed transformed, as if a calmer, quieter version of himself had emerged from behind the mask. He paced the walls, trailing his finger along the faded paper. '"As Hades and the dead are witnesses..."' He traced a dusty square. 'It was here,' he said, 'the painting. Antigone, the tragic Greek heroine. You know the story, Mrs. Christie? Sophocles wrote it as a play. Antigone risks her own life to give her brother a decent burial …' His voice tailed off. He stared at the wall, as if a painting still hung there, his eyes fixed on the ghostly outline. '"... with thrice poured drink offering she crowned the dead …"' He turned to Agatha. 'Her brother, a soldier, left dead after the war. Creon, the King, her Uncle, forbids her to bury him – in Creon's view, he deserves an ignoble death. But she goes back, you see … risks everything …' His voice cracked. Once more his gaze turned towards the blank, damp wall. 'They'll have taken it up to the big house, I imagine. Keep it safe …' He touched the wall, his finger drawing outlines on the peeling paper. '"Thy spirit hath fled, not by thy folly, but by mine own …"' He broke off, and turned to her, as if surprised to see her there. 'The worry is,' he said, as if talking to himself, 'the worry is, this darned biography written by that fool of a chemist. And now he's dead. The loose ends, don't you know, what's concealed, what's revealed. That's the thing about camouflage – it's either mimicry or disguise. You make something invisible, or you make it look like something it isn't.' A thin smile hovered round his lips. He began to pace the hall. 'Ghosts,' he said. 'The conversations. About art, and war, and courage. About the distinction between foolhardiness and bravery. The rules of art, the rule of law, the breaking of the rules …' He came to a halt in front of her. '"Dreadful is the mysterious power of fate; there is no deliverance from it by wealth or by war, by fenced city or dark, sea-beaten ships …"' He lurched towards her, and she was afraid he was going to take hold of her, but instead he loped past her, down a dark passageway, further into the house.

She followed him. They came out into a wide, open room. More peeling yellow walls, the cracked wooden floor, the dry leaves wafting gently as the door swung shut behind them.

'The studio,' he said. 'They were all here. If you could have seen it. A fire burning in the grate there, there were candles in holders on the walls –' He pointed at the circles of soot.

'Who were they?'

Again, the dazed look as he met her eyes. 'Artists. The French were ahead of us, the bonhommes, they were already established at the workshop in Amiens. But some of ours gathered here. Wilkinson, Tunnard, Chesney, even, before he went to France. Mind you, he fell out with them all, said a *camoufleur* had to be half soldier, half artist. He reckoned they weren't brave enough. If he only knew …' He was standing close to her in the damp chill of the room. She could hear his breathing. He spoke again. 'The war changed everything, Mrs. Christie. And it changed what we thought of as art. Broke all the rules. Now the artist asks more of you, the viewer. We ask you to look again, to look anew …'

He gazed at the wall, as if seeing the canvases still hanging there. Through the splintered glass of the windows came the sound of birdsong. At the corner of the floor was a rustle, of mice, perhaps.

'The war broke all the rules,' he said. 'For better and for worse.'

'We,' Agatha said. 'You said, when you were talking about artists, "we".'

'Did I?' He gave an empty smile.

She gazed up at him. 'What brought you here?' she said. 'When this house was inhabited, when it was full of talk, and warmth and light?'

He shook his head.

'Someone you knew?'

He flashed her a look.

'Someone who died?'

He flinched.

'We all lost people in that terrible war,' Agatha said. 'So much suffering. The casualties, the men I nursed. The damage.' She shook herself, stepped away from him. 'We should get back,' she said. She began to walk towards the door. 'Even cold ham begins to have a certain appeal.'

'I didn't bury him.' The words cut through the air behind her. She turned to face him. Mr. Farrar was white-faced, his fists clenched at his side. 'He was in the mud … there was blood, he was lying at a strange angle – that sound, that rattle, the dying breath, unmistakable … Come on, they were saying, they took hold of me, come away … There was gunfire …' He began to hit his fists against his legs. 'I tried to run back, but they grabbed me, marched me away. "For God's sake, man," they were saying, "you'll get yourself killed …"' His voice faltered. He was standing in the middle of the room, his eyes fixed, unseeing.

She took a step towards him. 'Who?' she asked, gently.

He appeared not to hear her. '"Woe for the sins of a darkened soul, stubborn sins, fraught with death …"'

'Mr. Farrar …' She touched his sleeve.

He gave a choking cry, slapped his hands over his eyes.

'We must go,' she said.

'He was left unburied. I loved him …' His words were barely audible. He stood, unmoving.

She put her hand to his elbow, and began to lead him, out of the room, along the darkened passage. His steps were shuffling, uneven beside her. She had a flash of memory, of taking a soldier's arm, knowing, as he limped at her side along the hospital corridor, that in the clean white walls he could see only the blood-soaked mud of the Somme.

She led Mr. Farrar into the hall, and, still holding his arm, opened the front door and pushed it wide open. There was sunlight, and she could see patches of blue in the sky. He stood, breathing hard, then released himself from her grip and stumbled out of the door. It was with relief that Agatha followed him.

Outside, on the golden stone of the front steps, he took several deep breaths. Then he turned to her, with an odd, exaggerated smile.

'Lunch,' he said. 'You're quite right. We should be just in time.' He leaned slightly towards her, and she prepared herself to take his arm again, but instead he made a sharp, military turn towards the rough side of the drive, allowing her the easier side as they walked back up the hill to the main path.

Chapter Eight

On their return to the hotel, Kurt managed to whisk them both into the kitchen entrance, unseen by the waiting reporters and newsmen. Once inside, he turned to her.

'I must apologise,' he said. He patted his pockets, drew out a packet of cigarettes.

They had walked back from Ince Hall in silence. The exertion seemed to have settled him. The colour had returned to his face. He lit a cigarette, inhaled deeply.

'You have no need,' she said.

'It won't happen again.'

'Mr. Farrar – it seems to me –'

'I appreciate your accompanying me to the house,' he went on. 'It means a lot to me, that building.' His tone was distant; the subject seemed to be closed.

'Perhaps one day you'll explain,' she said.

A clipped, polite smile behind a curl of smoke. 'I hope one day to be able to, Mrs. Christie. And now I must leave you to take luncheon alone. I do feel so responsible for Blanche. I promised her husband I'd look after her, and I fear I am shirking my responsibilities.'

Chameleon, she thought, looking at him. The dark anguish had gone, replaced with this artificial brittleness. He leaned towards her and took her hand in a formal grasp. Then he strode away along the carpeted corridor, all rangy, elegant ease.

How many, Agatha thought, as she turned to walk towards the dining room, how many of our men carry under a façade of normality the open wounds of war? A sudden image came to mind, her husband's medals set out in their glass cabinet, telling their own story of courage under fire.

I hope he got my telegram, she thought.

*

Lunch was being served with calm and order, as if there was no encampment of press outside or huddles of police on the tennis courts.

Mr. Finch gave Agatha a brief bow. 'Table for one?'

'Yes please,' she said.

'We need all the peace and quiet we can get at the moment,' he said, with a small smile.

Mr. Farrar had settled on a table with Mrs. Winters and Sophie. Agatha watched them, and thought how, rather than Kurt having to look after Blanche, all the evidence showed that it was she who was looking after him. There was a concern verging on fussiness, in the way she topped up his lemonade, the way she insisted on his having a second helping of salmon. Next to her sat Sophie, her plate untouched, her gaze drifting beyond the windows to the tennis courts with their bustle of police activity. From time to time the child would tear her attention away from the exterior and survey the room, as if looking for someone. Young Hughes, Agatha surmised, thinking what a shame it was that the girl had found a harmless romance of which she was now deprived.

'Where's the boy?' Kurt's voice cut through the room, as Finch approached their table.

Agatha winced at such an inappropriate conversational opening. She was aware of Blanche doing the same, a warning hand on Kurt's arm.

Kurt shook this off. 'We're missing him on this table,' he said.

Mr. Finch stood, stiff and correct. 'We felt that in the circumstances, Sir, it would be better for him to be elsewhere. Until all this blows over.'

'Up at the big house, eh?' Kurt flashed Finch a smile.

The manager gave a brief nod. 'Yes, Sir. Up at Langlands. The police have given Frau Adler permission to return home, and knowing her affection for the boy, I felt it was better for everyone if young Hughes stayed there for a while.' He reached for the empty serving dish and hurried away with it.

'Perhaps we'll visit him there.' Mr. Farrar had turned to Sophie, and this comment was addressed to her with a smile.

'You'll do no such thing.' Blanche's voice was sharp. 'How on earth do you think that would look? Turning up there unannounced – Ah, here's Sebastian.' The out-breath of relief was all too apparent, as Blanche moved her chair to make space for the tennis coach.

'So sorry I was delayed.' He took his place beside her. 'Our neighbourhood constable was cross-examining me about the layout of the tennis court. Seems to think I'm an expert.' He gave a bright laugh, and reached for a bread roll. He was in loose white trousers and a white blazer, his tie roughly fastened, as if added as an afterthought.

'I don't know how poor Sophie is going to improve her game in time, what with all that going on.' Blanche waved a dismissive arm towards the tennis courts.

'They'll be gone soon enough,' Sebastian said, taking the butter dish she passed him. 'A dead body is a dead body. There's a limit to what they can find out.'

'You'd be surprised.' It was Mr. Farrar who spoke.

Agatha was aware of a warning glance passing from Blanche to Sebastian.

'When it comes to dead bodies, I mean.' Kurt was still smiling, but there was a hollowness about his face.

'Kurt –' Blanche began.

'The stories a dead man can tell you...'

'Not now –' Blanche tried.

'Oh Uncle Kurt.' It was Sophie's light voice, cutting through his speech. 'Tell us later, not now.'

He blinked, stared at her.

'Tell us when we've got time to listen properly.' She reached out and took his hand in hers. He gazed at their hands, and a slow smile spread across his face. He nodded. 'When we've got time,' he repeated. Then he reached for another bread roll, and began to eat hungrily.

*

The dining room was filling up. Agatha found there were some guests she didn't recognize, and wondered whether a ghoulish fascination was bringing new customers. Two well-dressed, elderly ladies sat at one table. They were wearing almost identical tweed suits, and their conversation, in a refined Scottish accent, seemed to be mostly shrill disagreement.

Mr. Finch oversaw the service of lunch with his usual composure. There was no sign of Mrs. Collyer, but Mr. Tyndall had just arrived, alone, and was shown to his usual table. He didn't sit down, however, but began to pace the room, pink-faced and flustered.

'Cross-examined as if I were the murderer,' he said. 'Treated like some kind of criminal.' He had reached their two tables, and now addressed the space in between them. 'And poor Lillian questioned too. I'd only just arrived at the house and there they were, proceeding to treat her as if she was the killer. "Bolsheviks" was the word they used. No understanding at all, no allowances made. Her secretary and I had to intervene to prevent her being upset by their rudeness.'

Mr. Farrar was sitting bolt upright. His eyes were fixed on Mr. Tyndall, who continued, 'Implying that poor Frau Adler is some kind of revolutionary. She's simply a quiet English widow, living a quiet English life up there. You'd think things would have improved since the war. Any whiff of being foreign, or an artist, or both, and the police start voicing their clumsy suspicions ... Just as well Mr. Fitzwilliam was there. Calmed everything down. They wanted to see some papers, and he fished them all out, handed it all over.'

'Papers?' Kurt's voice was sharp.

Mr. Tyndall sighed. 'The man had no choice. The police seem to think that Frederick's biographical researches are of interest. Quentin found all the papers he could.'

'Have they taken them away?' Kurt asked.

'The police? Yes. Outrageous liberty if you ask me. I mean, what on earth do they hope to find, upsetting a respectable woman like Frau Adler ...'

Kurt was squeezing his fists against the table. Blanche put a warning hand on his arm.

Mr. Tyndall went on, 'Well, they're welcome to them. Can't imagine they'll draw any useful conclusions, those bumbling constables, treating us all as suspects –' He broke off, as Finch approached.

'Salmon, Sir?'

Mr. Tyndall seemed to breathe. He became calm, smiled, turned towards his table. 'Salmon, Finch. Thank you.'

The room settled into quiet conversation. Sebastian and Sophie discussed tennis. Mr. Tyndall ate in silence. After a while, Mrs. Collyer appeared, wraith-like in a cream-coloured gown. Finch was at her elbow, steering her towards her table, but she fluttered a hand in refusal, crossed the room to the piano and began to play.

The sun had emerged again, high in the afternoon sky, and the terrace was illumined with its rays. The notes of Chopin tinkled through the hubbub of the diners. Outside, the tennis courts cleared as the police moved their investigations on to the lawn. Sophie and

Sebastian got to their feet and headed out for a game, followed, surprisingly, by Kurt.

Agatha had bent to her notebook, and was beginning to write in it. A flurry of images circled, of medals and telegrams, misty railway stations and hasty goodbyes. The flowering of love. The past of the story which brings about the present –

'It's the gunshot.' Agatha looked up to find Blanche standing by her table. 'I must apologise for Mr. Farrar's bad behaviour. I do hope he hasn't been troubling you.'

Agatha sighed, and closed her notebook. 'No,' she said. 'Not at all. It's rather stressful for all of us,' she added.

Without being invited, Blanche took the seat at her table. 'I'm so sorry about his rudeness yesterday,' she said to Agatha. 'My husband is so fond of him, and when this idea for a holiday was suggested, we wanted to encourage him. Kurt so rarely relaxes, after what he's been through.' She leant back in the chair, her gaze following the tennis game in the stormy sunlight.

'Your husband didn't come with you?' Agatha asked.

'Oh no,' Blanche replied, with a girlish shake of her head, 'Jerry's always so busy in the City. I thought he might have joined us at the weekend, but I fear these goings-on will keep him away now. It's a shame, because he's very fond of Kurt, they're cousins, and they grew up together. Kurt's mother died young, you see, and so my husband's mother took him in when he was about fourteen, so they spent those precious years together, even their schooling.' Her gaze went to the tennis courts. Agatha could hear the soft bouncing of the ball, Sebastian's shouts of encouragement. Kurt was sitting on the grass at the side, leaning on one arm, watching.

'He's still like a child in many ways,' Blanche said. 'In spite of what he's gone through...'

'He was an artist?' Agatha asked.

Blanche flicked her a glance. She nodded. 'He was. Before the war. He studied in London. He was considered very promising, went around with some of the greatest talents of his generation. And then...' Her face clouded.

'The war,' Agatha said.

'So terrible. For so many of us.'

'So – the noise of the gunshot, on the tennis courts there –'

Blanche turned to her. 'I think it must have triggered something. A memory. I think it caused him to relive some past horror. I'm terribly worried that the police will read more into his behaviour than simply the concerns of an innocent but damaged man.'

'He was telling me about a painting,' Agatha said. Blanche gave a twitch of something like annoyance. 'Antigone,' Agatha went on.

'Oh that darned painting,' Blanche burst out. 'He saw it some years ago, in a house near here. Some old Greek tale about a silly girl who disobeys her uncle to sprinkle dust on some poor boy who's died in battle. It seems to mean something to dear Kurt.'

'Something about his own life?' Agatha prompted.

Blanche gave a shrug.

'Antigone broke the rules to bury her dead brother,' Agatha went on.

'As I said. A silly girl.' Blanche shifted on her seat.

'Mr. Farrar was telling me, about how the war changed the rules –'

'Rules exist for good reason.' There was a forcefulness in Blanche's tone. 'People shouldn't go breaking them.'

'He implied,' Agatha went on, 'that someone he knew had died. In battle, perhaps.'

Blanche turned to her. 'I know very little about it. All I know is, my husband's cousin came back from the war a changed man. He hasn't picked up a paintbrush since. Jerry thinks it would help him if he did.' She shifted her position to face the tennis court, and said no more.

*

The game progressed. Kurt seemed to be shouting out the scores. After a while he called up to Blanche, and she went out to join them. The sun dazzled across the tennis courts. On the horizon, the clouds gathered ready for another storm.

Agatha thought about Blanche's sweet concern for her husband's cousin. She reflected on Mr. Tyndall's outrage. She thought about Frau Adler, and Mr. Farrar's shock at encountering Quentin Fitzwilliam, the secretary. She saw in her mind the ghostly ruined manor house, heard again Mr. Farrar's recitation of Antigone, the girl who risks her life in order to bury the dead. She thought about the gaps where the paintings used to be, about Mr. Farrar's nervous collapse, his talk of art and broken rules.

She watched the unlikely tennis party, and wondered what had really brought them here.

Chapter Nine

The promised storm shrank to mere drizzle overnight, and the next day dawned calm and sunlit. The hotel too, seemed to be asserting normality, and breakfast was orderly and cheerful.

Agatha was breakfasting alone, her notebook at her side. From time to time she wrote in it. Yesterday it had occurred to her that Captain Wingfield would have to declare himself no longer engaged to the unsuitable fiancée, daughter of Lady Bertram, before he could honourably ask the governess for her hand in marriage –

'More tea, Madam.' Finch stood at her elbow with a large teapot. 'I've brought your newspaper too.' He poured her tea. Then, instead of moving away, he stood, stock still, staring across the room. 'I'm worried about that man,' he said, almost to himself.

Agatha followed his gaze.

Mr. Farrar was sitting, alone, a plate of eggs and bacon cooling on one side. In front of him was a stack of files, and he was leafing through them with a rather fretful eagerness.

'More of those papers from Mr. Collyer's research,' Mr. Finch said. 'The police took the ones from the Adlers' house, but these are a second set. He's convinced someone that he's the man to help. It's a terrible mistake.'

Agatha watched the feverish flicking of the papers. 'Who gave them to him?'

Finch hesitated. He spoke in a low voice. 'I would not normally dream of indulging in gossip, Madam,' he said. 'I speak only from concern. Mr. Farrar's mental state is not of the strongest. Like many young men after this terrible war ...' Again, he watched as Kurt turned page after page. 'I gather that he approached Mrs. Collyer last night, and offered to help. I think she was only too glad to get rid of the things. But in my view, if those papers do indeed hold clues to this awful killing, then Detective Inspector Olds needs to know what they say.'

'And do you think they do hold clues?' Agatha found herself gazing into his clear blue eyes.

Again, the hesitation. 'I'm sure the police know what they're doing. My main concern is that there is a murderer at large, and the sooner he can be caught the better.' He was looking directly at her, and now a new resolve crossed his face, as if he'd made a decision. 'Madam, I wonder if I might confide in you, perhaps later on this morning? It is not a liberty I would presume to take in normal circumstances, but with these terrible events ...'

'Yes,' she said. 'Of course.'

'I will be in my pantry, after the service of breakfast. If it's not too much trouble.'

She assured him that it was no trouble at all, and that she would find him there. She sat at her table and finished her breakfast, flicking through the *Times*.

She read about Egyptian tombs and the price of rubber. She studied a story about a missing girl from Dorset, a nursery-maid, who hadn't been seen for days. Her mother was beside herself with worry. They were trawling the local river with some arrangement of mercury and bread, the mercury buried in a loaf and dangled over the water. Agatha turned the page, scanned the death notices, put the paper down.

The room had gradually emptied. Kurt suddenly folded the files shut, tucked them all under his arm and hurried away.

*

Half an hour later, Agatha found herself knocking on the door of Mr. Finch's pantry.

It was a small, neat room, with a high window and a mahogany table at which were pulled up two chairs. Finch was sitting on one of them, and looked up at her with obvious relief. He gestured to the other chair, and she sat down.

He was silent for a moment, as if gathering his thoughts, as if unaccustomed to an interview of this nature. Then he spoke. 'I fear, Madam, that secrets were about to be betrayed. Secrets, perhaps, worth killing for.'

He sat upright, in clean, crisp white, with his open blue gaze. 'I wouldn't normally betray any of these confidences, but these circumstances have rather knocked my usual rules.' He took a breath, then said, 'Mrs. Adler and Mr. Tyndall are … are what one might describe as fond of each other. That in itself is no secret. However …' His words faltered.

In her mind, Agatha saw Mr. Tyndall, his care for Frau Adler, his springing to her defence.

Finch spoke again. 'Their close friendship, it is believed locally, predated the death of Dr. Adler.' He gave an out-breath of relief, as if unused to uttering such words.

'I see,' she said.

'I would not normally confide such things to a third party, but the thought that someone might evade justice due to my silence … it is not a comfortable thought.'

'No,' she agreed. Then she said, 'Have you told the police?'

He shook his head. 'I wanted to ask your advice before I did so.'

She looked at this man in front of her, his soft blond-white hair, his broad, reliable shoulders. She felt strangely flattered.

Directly above him hung a framed painting, painted in oils. It showed a mother with her children, the woman golden-haired in flowing blue, the two children, fresh-faced boys in sailor suits, encircled by her loving arms. An evocation of family life. It seemed further to sharpen the sense of loneliness about this man in front of her.

'Detective Inspector Olds,' she said. 'He's local, he told me. Perhaps he already knows this –' Gossip, she was about to say.

'Perhaps.' Mr. Finch looked as if this was unlikely.

'You think not?'

'It's difficult for you others to understand,' he said. 'There are ways, here, whereby people keep their secrets. My fear is that the secret was about to be betrayed. That's what brought about the danger. And to see Mr. Farrar with all those files from the big house sitting there in front of him, his breakfast getting cold … it made me feel a whole new fear.' He stopped, breathing, as if exhausted by so many words.

'I can see exactly what you mean,' Agatha said. She met his eyes.

'There is one other thing, Madam. I do so hate to burden you, but I really am beyond being able to see the right path …'

She waited. He went on, 'The revolver that was found, next to the body of poor Mr. Collyer … It is mine. A Weston Mark Six.'

'A soldier's weapon,' Agatha said, remembering Mr. Farrar's words.

He nodded. 'A soldier's weapon. A soldier. That's what I am.' A new weariness seemed to descend upon him. 'Oh, Madam. I have been going over and over in my mind, did I leave it loaded, how could I have left it here for anyone to steal? In my mind, I hear the firing of it, over and over …' His voice cracked.

'Mr. Finch,' she said. She reached out a hand as if to touch his arm, let her fingers rest on the table-top.

'I couldn't possibly have left it loaded.' His voice was agitated. 'Soldier's drill. The bullets were hidden. Someone must have found them …'

'Do the police know?'

He shook his head. 'I was about to confess to them.'

'Are you sure it's yours? It was a general issue weapon, I'm sure my husband had one –'

'My revolver has been missing from its place in that drawer ever since Monday. It was the first thing I checked.'

'Mr. Finch – if someone was determined to find your revolver, which they clearly were, nothing you did would have stopped them. And surely the police have found that the murderer loaded the weapon, not you.'

He nodded, mutely. 'I never left it loaded. Soldier's drill,' he repeated.

She withdrew her hand. 'Would you like me to mention this conversation to the police?'

His face seemed to soften with relief. 'Oh, Madam … if you would. It would mean I could sleep at night.'

He leaned towards her, as if about to shake her hand, then collected himself, and got to his feet, clicking his heels in a kind of salute. 'Madam, I am so grateful to you. An outsider, you see. If you tell them, it's not so bad.'

She stood up too. 'I do understand, Mr. Finch. I shall find that nice Detective.'

In the corridor he turned to her again. 'Thank you, Madam,' he repeated. 'You've rescued me.'

She smiled at him, and went on her way.

It was only when she was heading towards the tennis courts that it occurred to her that she had wanted to ask him more about young Oliver Hughes and his connection with Frau Adler.

*

There were no police to be seen throughout the hotel. Little May on reception told her they were all at the shipwreck – 'They've found gold there, Madam, that's what everyone was saying in the kitchen.'

It was a beautiful morning. Agatha imagined herself sitting in her room, gazing at the azure sea, writing the words whereby Captain Wingfield would declare his love to Martha Hobbes. With a sigh, she remembered her promise to Mr. Finch, that she would find Inspector Olds. She gathered her summer coat, and left the hotel.

She was unsurprised, as she neared the coast, to see others heading the same way. If they had 'found gold', she thought, it would bring people from far and wide. She could see the small Austin parked on the path, and sure enough, there on the beach was Inspector Olds, standing by the side of the shipwreck, deep in conversation with a man in a large fisherman's jumper and India-rubber boots.

She began to descend the steps, until at last her feet were on the shingle. The detective looked up as she approached, waved his pipe in her direction.

'Ah,' he said. 'Mrs. Christie. The rumours have reached as far as your ears, it seems. Bosun, this is Mrs. Christie. She's staying at the hotel where we've had our other trouble. Mrs. Christie, this is Bosun Ted Walker. He's been helping us with this monster here.'

Ted Walker was broad, brisk and bearded. He raised his hat, revealing shorn red-tinged hair. 'Pleasure, Madam,' he said, with a brief bow.

'I can only hope we're wrong.' Inspector Olds resumed their conversation. 'Treasure is the last thing we need. It was bad enough, with all the tales of ghosts.'

The Bosun smiled. 'It's a fishing boat. Why would it be carrying gold? At most, that chest will hold some kind of loot. We'll get it out and see what's what.' He turned back towards his team, with another tip of his cap. 'You're in safe hands, with my boys.'

The Detective watched him go, then turned to Agatha. 'I don't suppose you came in search of gold, Mrs. Christie?'

She smiled. 'No. I came because –'

'These events at the hotel,' he finished for her.

She nodded. 'I've had a conversation with the Hotel Manager, Mr. Finch.'

'Ah. Finch.'

'He – he wanted to confide in me, something that was on his mind.'

The policeman's eyes were fixed on her.

'He said,' she went on, 'that the, um, close friendship between Frau Adler and Mr. Tyndall … he said, he has reason to believe that it pre-dated the death of Dr. Adler. He was, as you can imagine, very embarrassed to be revealing such confidences, but he felt, in the circumstances, that it might be helpful. He wanted me to tell you.'

The policeman's gaze seemed to crystallise with dawning understanding. 'Ah,' he murmured.

'I did think perhaps it was the sort of gossip that the village already knew,' Agatha was saying.

He shook his head. 'No,' he said. 'I knew Mr. Tyndall was a friend of the couple. I didn't think ...' Again, the look of clarity. 'Ah,' he said again.

In front of them, activity. Hands digging, arms carrying, stacking. Beyond, the sea, sparkling in the sunlight.

Inspector Olds took off his hat and rubbed the back of his head. 'It's very helpful of Mr. Finch,' he said. 'But I'm not sure it sheds any light at all on the terrible death of Mr. Collyer. The work of a police officer, Mrs. Christie, is all about establishing the facts, not allowing oneself to be distracted. And the way I do that, is by following my intuition. I mean, to be sure, we have our methods, we can analyse the scene of the crime, we have all sorts of forensic tools … but for me, my intuition is at the heart of it all. Gut instinct, you might say.' He paused, scanning the activity at the Lady Leona. 'There is no doubt,' he went on, 'that someone wanted to silence Mr. Collyer. Of that I'm sure. But even if Mr. Collyer had uncovered some secret that Mrs. Adler and her friends didn't want uncovered, we still have to ask, is it for that that he was silenced? Or is it something more?' He turned to her. 'There's an old manor house, over towards the woodland. It's derelict now. But during the war, it was a centre for all kinds of goings on.'

'Ince Hall?' she asked.

He blinked. 'Yes,' he said, watching her. 'Ince Hall. You know it?'

Agatha spoke reluctantly. 'Mr. Farrar brought me there yesterday.'

His eyes narrowed with interest. He drew on his pipe, though it seemed to have gone out. 'Ah. Mr. Farrar.'

'You think it's connected to the murder?' she asked.

He paused, as if calculating how much to say. Then he spoke. 'This is what I think, Mrs. Christie. I think poor Mr. Collyer had stumbled upon a local connection in his work that led him into danger. Frau Adler then tried to stop him researching any further, whether out of concern for his well-being, or for more sinister reasons. All these facts will be established on my next visit to Langlands.'

'I see.'

'Certainly,' he went on, 'what Mr. Finch has said does add a certain weight to my theory, now I come to think about it.'

'Young Hughes is at Langlands, isn't he?' Agatha said.

His face softened. 'Mr. Finch has sent him back there for safekeeping. Very wise, in my view.'

'He seems to care about him very much,' she said.

His expression exuded warmth. 'That poor boy had ended up with no one. His father died at Ypres. Brave man, he was. And then his mother was very poorly, after the war. You'd see her, creeping to the shops here. Grief, my wife said. They said influenza, but my Elsie always said it was sorrow. And then poor Oliver had no one else. Finch has taken him under his wing. He's a very caring man,' he said. 'Have you noticed how his staff are devoted to him? His men were the same, during the war. Devoted.'

A shout came up from the shipwreck. A man, taller than the others, was emerging from the bones of the ship, carrying a large chest. There were more shouts, laughter; people downed tools and gathered around him.

'There we are, then. Moment of truth. I'd better get my men on guard just in case it's gold after all.' Inspector Olds gave a smile.

'And then it's up to the big house.' He began to walk towards the ship. 'Mr. Farrar, eh? I might have to have another word with him. If it turns out he knew something about the goings-on at Ince Hall, we may be getting somewhere. It's an inescapable fact that he was first on the scene of the crime. These things matter, you know.'

Agatha followed him towards the listing hulk. A crowd had gathered around the chest. Sergeant Brierley was standing beside Bosun Walker. The villagers were producing tools to prize open the chest, which was square and large and seemed to be made of metal.

Agatha turned to Inspector Olds again. 'There's one more thing,' she said. 'About the murder weapon.'

Inspector Olds looked at her.

'Mr. Finch said that the pistol that you found on the tennis courts was his. War Office standard issue, apparently.'

Inspector Olds smiled at her. 'Madam, I had concluded that myself. This murderer, whoever he is, is no fool. He would have made sure the weapon left no clue. Discovering the unloaded pistol in the butler's pantry, it would have been a matter of minutes to load it, seize his moment on the tennis courts, and then drop the weapon and disappear. We are having it tested for fingerprints. I had already surmised, that, should it carry any prints, they would include those of Mr. Finch. I shall reassure him when I next see him. And, more importantly, I will have another chat with Mr. Farrar and the others. Facts, you see, Mrs. Christie. Always establish the facts.' He took a match from his pocket, re-lit his pipe. 'Of course,' he went on, 'There is always the alternative conclusion, that we might yet be looking for a killer who has long since fled. And that will make my work a lot more difficult.'

There was another roar from the crowd, as the lid of the half-rusted chest was at last prized open. Then there was jostling, shouting, and, at last, cries of 'Empty!'

'Empty,' Inspector Olds repeated. 'I'm afraid I'm not at all surprised. Well, this makes my job a little easier, I hope.' He turned to her and offered his hand. 'I wish you a good afternoon, Mrs. Christie.'

*

Captain Wingfield slipped away from the empty chatter of the drawing room through the French windows. He found himself in the garden, and noticed, not for the first time, how clipped it appeared, as if the splendour of the flowers was being deliberately tamed. Wandering further away from the house, in the warm afternoon sunlight, he came upon the walls of the old garden, with the grey stone sundial at their centre. Here the wild roses rambled, tangled in a blaze of colour. He listened to the birdsong; but there was another sound, that of a woman weeping. And there he espied Miss Hobbes, seated on a stone bench, quietly sobbing.

'Miss Hobbes,' he said, approaching her. 'Whatever is the matter?'

She shook her head, saying only, 'I wish you every happiness.'

'My dear,' he said. What are you talking about?'

She raised her pretty face to him. 'Your engagement,' she said. 'To Peggy Bertram.'

Captain Wingfield felt the breath go out of him as he registered his surprise. 'Miss Hobbes,' he said. 'Please disabuse yourself of such an idea. I'm not engaged. To Miss Bertram or to anyone else for that matter.'

Now it was Miss Hobbes' turn to show astonishment. 'You're not to be married?' she asked.

'My dear Miss Hobbes,' he said. 'If I'm to marry anyone, it will be you.'

Agatha put down her pen, and re-read her words. She got to her feet and went out on to the balcony of her hotel room. The sunshine had persisted into the afternoon, and a calm had returned to the hotel. Tennis was being played on the tennis court again. It was beginning to feel like a normal holiday. She thought about her telegram to Archie. It all seemed rather over-dramatic now. Perhaps that's why he hadn't replied, because he knew there was no need.

Inspector Olds was presumably up at Langlands again. She decided to reassure Mr. Finch about the murder weapon, and went to find him.

There was no sign of the hotel manager anywhere. His pantry was empty. Wandering back towards the Palm Court she encountered, instead, Mr. Farrar. He was striding towards her, a stack of files clutched across his chest.

'Hah!' he said. 'Just the woman I wanted to speak to.'

Agatha felt a sinking feeling. Captain Wingfield's proposal to Miss Hobbes was still unwritten. She wished she hadn't left her desk.

'The police,' he said. 'Bound to question me. Blanche is terribly worried, mental state, you know, all a bit fragile.' He stood in the corridor, shifting his weight from foot to foot.

'I'm sure they don't think you're a suspect, Mr. Farrar.'

'Shall we consider the facts, Mrs. Christie?' His voice was loud in the soft carpeted space. 'On the morning of the murder, a gunshot is heard, at six or thereabouts. It is known that I had arranged to play tennis with the deceased. It is also known that the only two people present on the courts at the point where the staff run out to see what's going on, is me, and Mr. Collyer. Mr. Collyer is dying, from a single gunshot wound. And there I am, standing there on the tennis court. It is quite clear that I am the only person in this hotel with no alibi. Everyone else has proved that they were elsewhere. The chambermaids were stoking the fires for hot water. The cooks were in the kitchen, and the front of house staff were preparing for breakfast service, along with young Oliver and Mr. Finch, all tucked away behind the green baize door. Mrs. Collyer was roused by the noise. And Mr. Tyndall claims he slept through it, though I have reason to doubt that.'

'You do?'

He looked into the distance, then back at her. 'He seemed to be up and dressed in record time, shall we say, for someone who claimed to be asleep at the time of the shooting. But Mrs. Christie, all this is the sort of evidence that, in your stories, proves to be of great importance.'

He was fidgety and nervous, his arms still holding the files. Agatha laid a hand lightly on his arm. 'Shall we go and find a cup of tea, Mr. Farrar?'

They sat in the Palm Court, which was empty. The sunshine must have drawn people out to the terraces, Agatha thought, with relief. Little May served them, still full of stories of the shipwreck, 'Well, yes, Ma'am, you say the chest was empty but it might have had a hidden base, people are saying now, they want to saw it open if they can find the right tools, and in any case, there's another floor to the ship, there's every chance they'll find something there ...'

She placed the tray of tea things on the table, next to a copy of the *Times*. When she had gone, Agatha turned to Mr. Farrar. 'Are you saying to me that you really were standing by the dying man at the moment when the staff ran out?'

He stirred two large lumps of sugar into his tea.

'I can tell you what I know,' he went on. 'That I heard the gunshot. That for some reason, I ran towards it, rather than away. That I saw the body of Mr. Collyer, and, and ...' His face clouded. 'Mrs. Christie – I distinctly remember staring at my hand, and seeing the pistol grasped between my fingers.'

She looked at him. 'Mr. Farrar ...'

He waved away her words. 'In truth, Mrs. Christie, that is what I remember. More than that, I can't say. I remember knowing that I needed a drink.'

The files were piled on a chair beside him. He patted them with one hand. 'And the insane thing is, Mrs. Christie, for what? For what was the man killed? Have you read these things?'

He reached for the first file, opened it, pulled out an untidy sheaf of papers. He began to read. '... this century has already seen great progress made in the variegation of zinc sulfide seals ... With his subsequent work on cobalt salt stabilisation, Dr. Ernst Adler made many advances in the field of pigment chemistry ...' He flicked over a few pages. '... in this way, the neutral anionic clusters formed are resistant to oxidation...' He flung the paper down. 'How will that lead anyone to a murderer?'

'Mr. Farrar – Mr. Collyer was a chemist. He's bound to write chemistry.'

He allowed himself a small smile. 'But Dr. Adler ... Oh, Mrs. Christie, if you only knew.' He took a sip of tea, put down his cup. 'Have you ever looked into the eyes of a moth, Mrs. Christie? The eye of a moth reflects back hardly any of the light that it encounters. It's all to do with the wavelength of visible light. That's what they were working on. Paint that would absorb light rather than reflect it.'

'For the war effort?' she asked.

He nodded.

'At Ince Hall?' she prompted.

Again a nod. He spoke again. 'The eye of a moth is a thing of extraordinary beauty. It may be that to a mere chemist, it shows only the chemical composition of compounds capable of light absorption. But an artist sees light, colour, structure, meaning, feeling. From what I know of Dr. Adler, he was capable of both. An extraordinary man, by all accounts. And not just him, all of them. Oh, if you knew what those chaps actually did …'

'And what did they do, Mr. Farrar?'

She noticed, once again, the far-away expression in his eyes.

He sipped his tea, seemed to focus once again. 'Mrs. Christie,' he began. 'There is the truth of war. And then there are the stories we tell ourselves afterwards. Heroism. Winners. Victors. The Happy Ever After. The men who gathered at Ince Hall had only one aim in mind, to serve their country. Half of those chaps are no longer with us. Shot down, two of them, flying over enemy lines. Your husband will know about that. Another two lie cold and still in the fields of Flanders. There is no justice. When we talk of the soldier's death, the honourable death, we're lying to ourselves. That's all. It's no more than one of your thin fictions, Mrs. Christie.'

She found herself gathering words in defence of her own work, but he was speaking again. 'There is no sense. No resolution.' He had snatched up the copy of the *Times*. 'This is your reality.' He waved the newspaper at her. 'That girl they're looking for in Dorset, trawling the rivers, doing witchcraft with bits of bread to find her. Nursery maid they say she was. They'll find her body. Or they won't. Whatever happens, there will be no sense, no justice. Just some poor mother weeping quietly for her daughter. That's your reality. Rough edges, Mrs. Christie. No happy ever afters.' He flopped the paper back on to the table, picked up his cup and slurped at it roughly. 'They'll ask me about the tennis game, of course.

About why I'd invited Mr. Collyer to meet me early on Tuesday to play a few sets.'

'And why did you, Mr. Farrar?'

He flashed her a sharp glance. 'Oh, Mrs. Christie. Do you think I don't see through you? Another layer for your story-telling? It's not a game, Mrs. Christie.'

She was aware of a wave of a rage. 'I have never for one moment asserted that it was a game,' she said, trying to keep her voice calm.

He seemed not to hear. 'Your stories with your neat rows of suspects,' he went on. 'It's just divertissement,' he said.

'I make no great claims for my work.' Her voice was tight. 'People enjoy detective fiction, that's all.'

'No grief. No loss. No rage. Nothing real. Just a parlour game, a body in the library, a murder at the vicarage. It's all just spillikins in the parlour. Next you'll be telling me the Butler did it. That's what usually happens in these sort of stories.' He clunked his cup on to the table and stumbled to his feet. 'In fact, there we are. Finch.'

'He's not a butler,' Agatha said.

'Hotel Manager then. They had that argument the night before Frederick died, didn't they?'

'Over a steak,' she said. 'You wouldn't kill for that.'

He gave an empty smile. 'Perhaps there's more to it. Perhaps he's a secret enemy, spying for the Bolsheviks, disguised as a butler?'

'Mr. Farrar – this is a real death. As you have so rightly pointed out, there is a widow's grief. And you accuse me of playing games?'

His gaze was locked with hers. His eyes blazed darkly.

Notes of music floated across the room from the piano. Nora was sitting at the keys, her soft white fingers shaping their tune. It seemed to be a kind of folk song, and after a moment Nora began to sing gently, a sorrowful air about a young man returning from war.

Kurt turned and watched the playing. Something about the melancholy notes, the soft singing voice, shifted his mood. He turned back to Agatha, all anger gone. He cast her a look of humility, struggled to find words. At length he said, 'Mrs. Christie ... My apologies. I am so used to people around me making allowances. It won't happen again.'

He bowed, clicked his heels and then left the room. Agatha listened to the lilt of the song, the final verse revealing that the soldier was a ghost, brought back by love alone. She heard the fragments of the words, the poetry of grief and loss. She thought about the shipwreck on the beach beyond.

Chapter Ten

Captain Wingfield considered the sundial, reflecting upon the creeping shadow that marked the passage of time itself. Despite the brightness of the day, he was haunted by a sense of heaviness...

At the ring of the dinner bell, Agatha put down her pen. She went to the dressing table, fastened her pearls around her neck, pinned back her hair.

There was still no reply from Archie. It occurred to her, as she stared at her reflection in the looking glass, that she could just go home. Home is where I belong, she thought, by my husband's side, not caught up in this very odd story of war artists and ruined manor houses, of shipwrecks and papers and ghosts, of tennis games that end in tragedy.

Perhaps my novel would be making more progress if I were back home, she thought. Back at my own study, with all my notebooks, and with dear Carlo sorting things out. Most of all, with Rosalind, she thought. I've been away from her too long.

In her mind, a picture of her daughter, playing with her cousins. There'd be ball games no doubt, laughter, hide and seek in the gardens, running, jumping, her daughter dancing, her golden curls shining in the sunlight...

I've been away too long.

She got to her feet, headed for the door. Tomorrow, she thought, I will find Inspector Olds and make sure I have his permission to leave.

*

The calm that had descended over the hotel earlier now seemed to be fractured. The mood in the dining room was tense, not helped by the shrill voices of the two Scottish ladies. Agatha took her place, and almost at once Mr. Finch was at her side. 'Madam,' he said, in a low voice, 'my thanks for your intervention. The Detective Inspector has put my mind at ease.'

She smiled, uttered a few words, 'Really it was no trouble, least I could do …' and then he had gone.

The tennis party appeared rather twitchy. Blanche sat with Sebastian and Sophie. From time to time she would lean over and insist that Sebastian tell her the time from his pocket watch.

'What can they want with him, all this time?' she said to Sebastian. 'I've got poor Finch keeping his dinner warm for him too.'

'Perhaps Uncle Kurt did it,' Sophie said. Her voice was tight, and she was drumming her fingers against the table.

'Don't be silly, dear,' Blanche said.

'He was awake at the same time as Mr. Collyer, wasn't he,' the girl went on. 'Completely unlike him. And in tennis shoes. No one else was on the courts at the moment that Mr. Collyer was killed, that's what the policeman said.'

Blanche opened her mouth as if to dispute this, but the girl's words carried an obvious, inarguable truth.

Sebastian laughed. 'You forget that dear Kurt has no motive. No motive at all.'

'Whereas I –' the voice was loud, as Robin Tyndall crossed the threshold into the dining room. 'I, it seems, have every motive. According to our local police officers.'

The tennis party looked up at him. The two Scottish ladies continued their loud conversation.

He marched to his table, his stick tapping loudly with each step. 'Vladimir Ilyich Lenin,' he said, his voice still loud. 'The man is no longer even with us, but any scrap of interest in him and you're treated as if you're firing up the tin-miners of Cornwall for imminent revolution. Fingerprints!' he exclaimed, loudly. 'They took my fingerprints! As if I'm some kind of lowly criminal ...' He flung himself into his chair, poured himself a large glass of wine and began to drink it.

There was the clink of plates, the pouring of drinks. Tyndall said no more. Blanche continued to watch the door, barely tasting her soup, tearing her bread into pieces, leaving it untouched.

Then, a swish as the door opened, and Kurt appeared. Blanche seemed to breathe again.

He was pale, distracted. He lumbered to the table and sat down, without speaking. Blanche flashed him a question in her eyes, but he ignored it. He reached for a bread roll, tore off a large piece and placed it in his mouth.

Sebastian turned to Sophie, and with great deliberation began a conversation about her opening serve.

Blanche murmured something to Kurt.

'… it's the placing of your feet, Sophie, you need that real strength, you need to ground yourself …' Sebastian was saying.

Blanche spoke again. Kurt turned to her, wearily. 'Of course I'm a suspect,' he said, loudly. 'I was there, wasn't I? In tennis kit, wasn't I? He's like a terrier, that policeman. Won't give up. Taking my fingerprints, as if that's going to give him any answers.' He swivelled round to face Mr. Tyndall. 'So, Tyndall,' he said. 'Which of us is it? One of us killed the poor man.'

Robin Tyndall faced him from his table. 'This is no joke, Farrar,' he said. 'What I want to know is, why did you insist on taking Frederick's papers?'

'The papers?' Kurt let out a bark of laughter. 'Mr. Collyer's tedious scrawls … as if that would tell me anything at all. The real disputed papers must be with the police by now, the ones they took from Frau Adler. All I've read is sleep-inducing lists of conferences attended by chemists, names of people who attended, formulae of chemical compounds …' He gave an exaggerated yawn. 'If anyone wanted to kill because of Mr. Collyer's writings, it would simply be to prevent themselves dying of boredom.'

'Kurt –' Blanche's voice was sharp. 'That really is enough. Have some respect.'

'What do you think, Tyndall?' Kurt ignored her. 'Where do you think the clue really lies? Up at the big house, perhaps? With Frau Adler? Or on the beach, in the middle of the night? With people waiting in the darkness for a ship to come in?'

Mr. Tyndall's face was ashen pale, his lips set with rage.

'Or maybe not there,' Kurt went on. 'Maybe it's that heap of crumbling golden stone further along the coast? You know the house, don't you, Tyndall? Perhaps it's there, under the old slate roof, mixed up with those broken dreams and shattered hopes. Perhaps it's there, the clue to this death, tangled up with all those other lives cut short?'

The air seemed to freeze. Even the two ladies had fallen silent. Blanche looked as if she was near to tears. Sebastian stared at his plate.

Mr. Tyndall rose to his feet. He placed a hand on the table to steady himself, and his voice shook with feeling. 'Mr. Farrar,' he said. 'I have had enough of this. There is one way to put a stop to these rumours, these rumours of rumours.' He took a white handkerchief from his pocket. 'Tomorrow –' He paused, dabbed at his forehead with the handkerchief. 'Tomorrow, we will go to see Frau Adler. We will take the forces of law and order with us. To Langlands,' he said. 'We will go together. I will put a stop to this calumny. All this talk of midnight ships, of poor Frau Adler waiting for contraband ... I will not have that poor woman's name dragged into this. Twice now, the police have questioned her. Her husband, Dr. Adler was an eminent chemist, blameless, as is his wife. I will request that the Inspector returns there with us, and I will put an end to speculation of this kind.'

Mr. Farrar stared up at him. After a moment he gave a nod of agreement. 'But,' Mr. Farrar added, 'I will take a witness. Mrs.

Christie here –' He pointed across the room – 'I will take Mrs. Christie here as an impartial observer.'

Mr. Tyndall looked across at her. 'Agreed,' he said. 'If you are, Mrs. Christie?'

In her mind, her daughter, her husband, her own desk, her notebooks, the lilac tree in her garden. In her mind, her writing, the easy flow of her own story, not the jagged edges of this one.

In the corner of the dining room stood Mrs. Collyer. She had slipped through the doorway and now stood, watching, her fingers twisting together, her wide eyes staring at Agatha with a look of pleading.

Agatha looked at Mr. Tyndall, and then at Mr. Farrar. 'Agreed,' she said.

*

The wind was up in the morning. Agatha was glad of the roof on the Detective Inspector's old Austin. She sat on the back seat. Mr. Farrar was sitting next to the Inspector, in the front seat, silent as a statue. She was glad of that too.

Inspector Olds had come to collect them from the hotel. 'Very kind of you, Mrs. Christie,' he'd murmured, holding the car door open for her. 'Mr. Tyndall is meeting us there with Brierley …' He'd started the engine, climbed into the driver's seat.

Blanche had stood on the hotel steps, seeing them off. She'd seemed almost tearful. 'Oh do look after him, Mrs. Christie,' she'd said. 'I'd come myself, but I think I'd be one person too many …'

She had waved an elegant hand, as the car had pulled away down the drive.

Langlands was a large, imposing house set in well-tended gardens, not far from the village itself.

Frau Adler had come to the door at the sound of the car engine, and now stood there, smart as ever, in a long tweed skirt and fine woollen shawl, with two small dogs yapping at her ankles.

'Mrs. Christie ... Mr. Farrar ...' She shook their hands, ushered them into the house. The dogs jumped at their legs, and she admonished them quietly. 'Jack Russells of course, wonderful company but no manners.' She smiled a thin smile. 'We're in the library. Robin's already here.' She seemed tense and chilled, as she gathered her shawl around her and led the way towards a double-door of heavy oak.

Mr. Farrar seemed not to hear, standing, immobile, in the middle of the hall. His eyes were fixed on a painting which hung next to the large staircase. It showed a woman in a white robe, kneeling by the body of a young man. The man's eyes were vacant with death, his flesh waxy. The woman's hands were held aloft, filled with earth, and her face was ashen with grief. Behind her, at a distance, a second, male figure, black-haired, dark-robed, taking a step towards her, his arm stretched out in a gesture of protest.

Kurt Farrar raised his hand to it, traced a finger along the lines of the dead body. 'A slain man's blood,' he murmured. He turned slightly towards Agatha. 'This is the painting,' he said. 'Antigone ...'

Frau Adler was standing by the double doors.

Kurt Farrar turned to her. 'You got it back,' he said. 'You rescued it. How …?'

Her gaze was level. 'It had to be done,' she said.

'Quentin …?' he asked.

She gave a small nod.

'Did he get them all?'

She shook her head. 'Ach, if only. It has been so hard, so, so hard. And with so much disagreement … but dear Quentin will not give up.' Her voice faltered with emotion.

'Brave man,' he said. 'Brave, brave man.'

'There's a grave now, Quentin says. Over in France. A good, proper marked grave …'

'For the fallen? For all of them?'

She nodded. Their eyes were locked for a moment, then she turned away. Mr. Farrar followed, and they all went into the library.

*

The party settled themselves around a long polished table. A young woman in starched white served small cups of strong black coffee. Frau Adler spoke to her in German, appeared to ask for sugar, as a few moments later she reappeared with a bowl and some spoons.

Inspector Olds sat at the head of the table, his sergeant at his side, notebook at the ready. Frau Adler was on his right, Mr. Tyndall opposite, his stick by his seat, and then Mr. Farrar and Agatha.

Inspector Olds took a reluctant sip of coffee. Then he spoke. 'I don't need to pretend to you all that things aren't serious. Mr.

Collyer seems to have had no enemies. He was an ordinary man, a chemist. He loved his subject. He admired your husband, Frau Adler, and as we know, he was writing his biography. And that's what we've gathered here to discuss.' He glanced at his coffee cup but didn't venture another sip. 'The feeling is, Frau Adler, that Mr. Collyer had stumbled upon an aspect of Dr. Adler's life that, shall we say, certain parties wished to be hidden.'

There was a slight quiver in his voice. It was clear that Inspector Olds was facing a situation completely new to him, and probably rather uncomfortable.

'Our investigation centres on three things,' he went on. 'Firstly, the events at the hotel on the morning of Mr. Collyer's untimely death. Secondly, the house further along the track there, Ince Hall. And thirdly, the actual papers belonging to Dr. Adler that Mr. Collyer had come to possess. Now, what we know is that a lot of people were up unreasonably early on the morning of Mr. Collyer's death. Not only Mr. Farrar here, but you, Frau Adler, you appeared at the hotel, having been driven there by your secretary. Do you have an explanation for that?'

Lilian Adler seemed pale with cold, perhaps, or from the tension that hung in the room. She put down her cup of coffee and said, 'It is simple. The papers. Frederick was about to betray secrets. I wanted the papers back. I still want them back. I was lucky that my friend here got wind of it.' She indicated Mr. Tyndall, with a small wave of her ringed fingers.

'And what exactly were those secrets, Frau Adler?' Inspector Olds' gaze was intense. Detective Sergeant Brierley too was waiting, pen poised in his hand.

Frau Adler gave a sigh. 'Ach, if only I knew. My husband was an admirable man. Admirable. I miss him terribly, as Mr. Tyndall here knows.'

Robin Tyndall gave a nod of his head.

'We are outsiders,' Lilian Adler went on. 'Everyone knows that. We were German, living here during a war with Germany. But our loyalties have always been to the country we called home. This country. Our children are Englishmen. My husband's work was on behalf of this country. His work on reflective paint, his art that made use of it to protect our soldiers in the Great War, all was out of loyalty to Britain, patriotism. And it is true, that during the war, Ince Hall was a hive of activity. The man who owned it was an artist too. He died, leaving no heirs. It continues to be disputed. That's why it has fallen into ruin.'

The policeman looked thoughtful. 'Ince Hall,' he said. 'Once owned by the Munro family?'

Lillian gave a small nod. 'Theodore Munro had inherited it,' she said. 'The painter.' She seemed about to say more, but Robin Tyndall threw her a warning glance.

Kurt Farrar was clutching the edge of the table. Agatha heard him murmur the name, 'Theodore.'

The Inspector took up his questioning again. 'Mr. Tyndall,' he said. 'Mr. Farrar. Could you explain how you know each other?'

111

They spoke at once. 'We don't,' Mr. Tyndall said, firmly. 'Artists,' Mr. Farrar said, across him.

The policeman looked from one to the other. 'Perhaps you could be a bit clearer?'

Robin Tyndall waited for Mr. Farrar to speak. Kurt glanced at Agatha, and then said, 'Mr. Tyndall was at Ince Hall, during the war.'

All eyes were on Robin, who inclined his head and said, 'That is correct.'

'He never saw active service,' Kurt went on.

'That is also correct. I had polio as a child, and it left me disabled. Also,' he added, 'I was getting on a bit by the time war was declared.'

The Inspector addressed Mr. Farrar. 'And you, Sir, were also at Ince Hall?'

'Only at the beginning. I was called up as a soldier. Devonshire Regiment, First Battalion. Mr. Tyndall arrived after that. As did Dr. Adler. I never met him. '

'That is correct, too,' Mr. Tyndall said.

'So –' The Inspector tucked his thumbs into his waistcoat – 'that still does not explain how you know each other.'

There was a moment of silence. Then Frau Adler spoke. 'Mr. Farrar has come here on holiday, have you not? Re-tracing memories of Ince Hall? You've encountered Mr. Tyndall from time to time that way.'

Kurt Farrar seemed to breathe. He nodded. 'Frau Adler is correct,' he said.

'You've stayed in the village before?' The Inspector eyed him closely. 'At the same hotel?'

'Once before,' Mr. Farrar replied. 'About a year ago.'

'Ah.' Inspector Olds tapped the notebook, watched his Detective Sergeant write it down. 'I have another question,' he said. 'What is the significance of these papers belonging to Dr. Adler? What might they conceal?'

A glance flashed between Tyndall and Frau Adler. Kurt Farrar began to speak. 'Inspector Olds ... I can tell you my fears surrounding Dr. Adler's papers. Dr. Adler was an expert on colour. His work on reflection and absorption of light proved invaluable in the development of pigments for use in camouflage. But he was more than just a chemist. He was an artist, too. He was a man of admirable qualities. I never met him, but, with your permission, Frau Adler, may I say how much his work was admired in his lifetime.'

She bowed her head in acknowledgement.

Kurt continued, 'It was entirely due to him that the artists who came to Ince Hall made such a huge contribution to the war effort. He was able to gather around him a group of chaps who became expert, not only in the tools of camouflage, but also in its application. We were sculptors, painters, cubists, pointillists ... We made periscopes that looked like trees, we made watchtowers that couldn't be seen from the sky, we made ourselves invisible ...' His face shadowed. 'I wasn't there for long, but it was a precious, privileged time.'

'And the papers?' the Inspector prompted.

Mr. Farrar sighed. He met his eyes. 'There are many casualties of war, Inspector. As I'm sure you know. Not just the dead, the wounded, the widowed, the orphaned. But there are also those who are silenced by the horrors they have seen. Dr. Adler allowed such people to bear witness. He listened to their tales of brutality, unfurled in fragments, words tumbling out between weeping. And then, he would paint. His sympathetic listening allowed these people's stories a shape, a colour. It allowed for beauty, for redemption.'

There was a silence, then Inspector Olds said, 'But you never met him.'

Kurt Farrar shook his head. 'I wish I had.'

'So the papers?' the Inspector prompted.

Frau Adler cleared her throat. 'If I may, Mr. Farrar …' She turned to the policeman. 'My husband knew of an event that took place, during the war, which concerned Mr. Farrar; an event of some tragedy. It may well be that buried within his possessions, there is some evidence of this tragedy.'

The Inspector looked from Frau Adler to Kurt Farrar. 'When you suggested to Mr. Collyer that you would teach him tennis, was it with this in mind?'

Kurt Farrar gave a small nod of agreement.

'And did you ever find out if Mr. Collyer had these papers, this evidence, in his possession?'

Mr. Farrar shook his head. 'No, Sir. I didn't.'

'Because the man was dead by then?'

Another brief nod.

'Since then, Mr. Farrar, you have persuaded Mrs. Collyer to lend you the papers in her possession?'

'Oh yes,' Mr. Farrar said. 'And now I know everything about white pigments and the Munsell Colour System. Hue, chroma, value ...' He smiled, and the tension in the room seemed to lift. Frau Adler leaned back a little, Mr. Tyndall settled in his chair.

The Inspector was gazing at the table top. He raised his head and addressed Mr. Tyndall.

'Mr. Tyndall, it is no secret that your political sympathies are, shall we say, extreme?'

Robin Tyndall gave a theatrical sigh. 'Oh, Inspector, are we to have more of this?'

'You encountered Dr. and Frau Adler some years ago?'

'Mr. Farrar has explained. I was living locally, I was drawn into the Ince Hall circle, and then became closer friends with the Adlers when they retired here.'

'You're known to have published letters in the local press concerning the political situation in Russia. Sympathetic letters –'

Mr. Tyndall interrupted the Inspector. 'It's not a crime, as far as I know, in this country, to express a political point of view in the newspapers.'

'No,' the policeman conceded. 'It's not. However –'

He broke off, as the door opened. Oliver Hughes stood there, shyly. He was pink-cheeked, bright eyed, wearing a neat suit in navy blue.

'Oliver, darling –' Lillian opened her arms and he went to her. 'Have you had a lovely day?'

'Yes thank you, Ma'am,' he said.

'Ach…' she gave a small laugh. 'Ma'am, he calls me.'

'I don't know what else to call you,' he said, blushing.

'Mrs. Adler, you called me, at the hotel. It made me smile. But before that, long before, you used to call me Bunty,' she laughed.

'I was little in those days.' He smiled up at her. 'But now I'm a grown-up. Bunty, Amy wants to know if she should serve more coffee in here.'

Lillian laughed. She glanced at Robin, then said, 'I don't think so. I believe the Inspector was just coming to the end of his questioning. Weren't you, Inspector Olds?'

At her side, Robin was gathering his stick, getting to his feet.

Inspector Olds surveyed the room, then appeared to concede. 'Indeed, yes. I have come to the end of my questioning.' He stood up, leaning on the back of his chair.

The party moved slowly into the hall. Lilian had an arm around Oliver, and was chatting to him, 'You must try one of the other horses tomorrow, Oliver, that little pony is too naughty, much too naughty…'

Kurt once more went to the painting.

'Antigone.' Agatha spoke to him, standing at his side.

He gave a nod.

'Did Dr Adler paint this?'

Again, a nod.

'Was this a witnessing,' she pursued. 'One of Dr. Adler's healing works?'

Another nod, barely perceptible.

Agatha pointed at the third character, the dark-haired man walking towards the heroine. 'Who's this?'

He turned to her. 'That's Haemon. He's the son of King Creon. He loves Antigone. He's due to marry her. When she is imprisoned, he kills himself. That's part of the tragedy, that Creon's rules bring about his own terrible loss, the death of his own son.'

'You said you never met Dr. Adler.'

'That's true.'

'So, this witnessing. This painting that helped a wounded soldier heal …'

Kurt's eyes were dark with feeling.

'This other man,' Agatha said. 'The man who loves Antigone, who tries to rescue her …' She glanced up at him, but his attention had gone beyond her, to the recesses of the hall. Agatha followed his gaze. Standing in the doorway, framed by its ornate green surround, was Quentin Fitzwilliam, the Adlers' secretary.

Agatha heard Kurt take a sharp gasp of breath. She looked at Mr. Fitzwilliam, his black hair and dark suit. She saw how unmistakable was the likeness between the secretary standing now before her, and Haemon, the grieving young man of the painting.

Chapter Eleven

Kurt Farrar's gaze was locked with that of Mr. Fitzwilliam. Lillian Adler had fallen silent and now watched, as Mr. Farrar turned hurriedly to leave, following the two policemen towards the front door.

Quentin Fitzwilliam raised a hand, as if to detain him, but Kurt had gone, hastening after the sergeant, who had gone out to the car.

Quentin, pale and shaking, turned and slipped away, back into the recesses of the house. Lillian watched him go, then rested her hand on the shoulder of young Oliver, who had come out to say goodbye to the party.

The Inspector bent to shake Oliver's hand. 'Goodbye young Hughes. See you in the village, perhaps.'

Oliver smiled, nodded.

Agatha found herself outside. The Inspector joined her by the car. On the steps, Robin Tyndall was standing next to Lillian Adler. The secretary was nowhere to be seen.

'May I offer you a lift back to the hotel, Mrs. Christie, Mr. Farrar?'

Inspector Olds' voice was cheerful. The sunlight shone on the paintwork of his Austin. Agatha hesitated. 'It seems our work here is done,' the Inspector was saying. He smiled at Sergeant Brierley. It was as if the rules had settled back to normal, as if now, out in the sunshine, everyone knew their place once more.

'Thank you,' Agatha said, following him towards the car.

'I'll walk,' Kurt said. 'If I'm allowed to.' He flashed a dry smile at the Inspector.

The policeman nodded his agreement.

'You know where to find me,' Kurt added, as he turned and headed away, down the drive.

Agatha got into the car. This time she sat at the front, next to the Inspector, with Sergeant Brierley driving. 'Mrs. Christie,' the Inspector said, once they were on their way, 'I have a favour to ask of you. As we know, Mr. Farrar persuaded Mrs. Collyer to hand over her husband's papers. In spite of all his talk of the dullness of the subject, I think they might well be useful. Particularly in the light of what we've learned today. So, once I've retrieved them, I wondered whether I could ask you to read them.'

Agatha agreed that she would be happy to read them. The Inspector's good mood seemed to grow with each turn in the road. By the time they approached the hotel, he was humming a tune.

At the hotel, Inspector Olds jumped out of the car and held the door open for her. As he did so, he said, 'Mrs. Christie, you might well be wondering why I let Tyndall off the hook. Well, I'll tell you. It's quite clear that the relationship he has with Frau Adler is not straightforward. Whatever gossip has been circulating, I fear it's true. And it's also clear, that whatever I would have asked him, I'd never have got a straight answer. But don't think I've finished with him, oh no. The man they call Bosun Walker has given me some very useful information on Mr. Tyndall's movements last Sunday night. Very useful indeed. I shall be following it up. Sergeant,' he called to Brierley, 'wait here while I raid Mr. Farrar's room for those papers.'

*

Half an hour later, Agatha was sitting in the Palm Court, with the heaps of files from Mr. Farrar's room in front of her. Inspector Olds had got the key from Finch, had swept them all off the desk, he told her, and had handed them over.

'I'll leave you in peace now, Mrs. Christie,' he said. 'You may be no detective, but I still appreciate your help in all this. Sometimes it can take a whole team of us, just getting to the facts.' He leaned back on his heels, surveying the files. 'There's no doubt that Mr. Tyndall has been involved in some kind of unauthorized shipping. I imagine, it's from those Soviets, some way of helping them with contraband, I'll wager. And I fear that Frau Adler is caught up in it too. I wouldn't be surprised if Mr. Farrar knows more than he's letting on. And the key fact is, Mrs. Christie, that Mr. Collyer had stumbled upon this information, and being a law-abiding sort of man, was about to reveal it.' He wagged a finger towards her. 'This is how we do it, we professionals. We have a method, and we allow the picture to emerge. Much as I appreciate your fictional version of our work, I'm sure you'd be the first to admit that it bears very little relation to real life. We have our methods, you see. We have our ways of getting to the facts. And one such fact is, Mrs. Christie, that the whole thing might be very simple. If Mr. Tyndall had reason to suspect that Mr. Collyer was about to reveal his affair with Frau

Adler, then there we are. He's here on the premises, he knew that there was this promised tennis lesson early that morning ... As I've said before, Mrs. Christie, these things are always about following one's intuition.' He'd shaken her hand with a warm smile, and then left.

*

Agatha sat with a pot of tea, leafing through the files. After a while she found herself agreeing with Mr. Farrar, that there was really nothing of interest in Mr. Collyer's notes, unless one was fascinated by the details of colour chemistry.

The good weather had persisted into the afternoon. The two Scottish ladies were taking tea on the terrace, and Agatha noticed Nora Collyer too, sitting outside at a shady table. She saw little May bring her a tray of tea, a plate of scones. Beyond the terrace she could glimpse the tennis party, poor Sophie hard at work practising her backhand.

There was a sense of anticipation, as if the whole hotel was waiting for something. The end of the story, Agatha thought. She had an image of Captain Wingfield, waiting too, for his own happy ending. The Captain's proposal of marriage would be more interesting than pigment stabilization, she thought.

She tucked the files under her arm and got to her feet. The final declaration of love between the Captain and dear Martha the governess would fill the time until dinner far more enjoyably than any more of Mr. Collyer's lists. She would simply have to agree with Inspector Olds that she was, after all, no detective.

*

Dinner took place with the same sense of subdued anticipation. Agatha was glad to be left alone, to leaf through the *Times* while eating a rather fine seafood salad. Mrs. Collyer was nowhere to be seen, but Blanche had said she'd intended to eat in her room. Agatha was surprised to see Mr. Farrar sitting with Blanche, Sophie and Sebastian. But he seemed listless, barely speaking. From time to time Blanche placed a concerned hand on his arm.

Agatha wondered, again, about Mr. Fitzwilliam. She thought about the dark-haired hero of the painting, the therapeutic bearing witness of Dr. Adler's art work. She finished her salad, glanced at the share prices.

'No sign of the poor nursery-maid, then?'

Agatha looked up to see Mr. Farrar standing at her elbow.

'No,' she agreed. 'Not yet.'

He pulled up a chair, flung himself into it. She noticed how drawn he seemed, his hair awry, his shirt unbuttoned at the neck.

'No happy endings, eh?' he said.

'Mr. Farrar ...' she began.

'The police raided my room, I gather,' he said. 'They've tasked you with those ghastly files.'

'Yes,' she said.

'Any luck?'

She shook her head. 'Just chemistry,' she said.

He smiled. 'As I say. No easy answers. I even checked up on our Butler story,' he said.

'Your Butler story,' she corrected him.

'I sneaked into Finch's office, trawled through his papers. All very disappointing. He really is just a butler. He's worked here for years, apart from war service. A brave soldier, mentioned in dispatches. Before that he was in a hotel in Fowey. Not a Bolshevik hair on his head.' He sighed. 'And, in any case, he was nowhere near the tennis courts at the moment of the murder. He is entirely accounted for, so the police say, tucked away in the kitchen, firing up the ovens, young Hughes at his side. So, Mrs. Christie. Here we are. Not a game at all. Just ordinary life. Just messy, disordered, meaningless …'

He was shadowed, edgy. She could see Mrs. Winters and the others leaving the dining room, but he showed no sign of joining them.

'Mr. Farrar,' she began.

'Quentin Fitzwilliam,' he said. He met her eyes. 'Is that what you wanted to ask me?'

'If you want to tell me,' she said.

He was drumming his long thin fingers on the table top. 'I thought perhaps you'd worked it out,' he said. 'A woman like you.'

'And what does that mean?' she asked him.

He gave an empty smile.

She looked at him. 'Mr. Fitzwilliam is a witness to your tragedy,' she said.

His gaze was level, but he said nothing.

'Someone you loved, who died in battle … and Mr. Fitzwilliam was there.'

A barely perceptible nod.

'And you feel responsible, somehow. Like Antigone, you feel that the right actions weren't carried out. A kind of guilt.'

His lips were working. His fingers still tapped against the table.

'But this was war, Mr. Farrar. The rules were different –'

'Guilt!' The word burst from him. 'Antigone broke the rules.' His voice cracked with anguish. 'The rules were unjust. I should have gone back. I should have buried him …' He covered his face with his hands.

Quietness settled around them. The dining room was empty, the tables cleared.

Agatha spoke again. 'Mr. Farrar – how did Quentin Fitzwilliam end up at Langlands?'

He lowered his hands and faced her. 'Art,' he said. 'Ince Hall was our studio. We lived together, we worked together. We grew to love each other …'

'When you say "we" – Quentin was one of these men?'

He nodded.

'And the other, was the owner of Ince Hall, Theodore Munro.'

He gave a flinch at the name. 'Yes,' he murmured.

'Was it he who gathered you all?'

Another nod.

'And then war came, and you were called up to serve. And Dr. Adler became part of the work at Ince Hall, as all that artistic skill was deployed in camouflage?'

'Yes,' he said.

'And some of these *camoufleurs* went to France?'

'Yes,' he said.

She took a breath, then went on. 'You joined them, at Amiens, perhaps? And Theodore, and Quentin, and you, served together? Until Theodore was killed –'

'Theodore,' he said. His voice was a monotone. 'I'd been telling him to hurry, we both had, Quentin and me.' He was staring straight ahead, as if she wasn't there. 'We were hungry, soaking wet, cold to the bone. We thought we were behind the lines. You could hear shelling. He was weak by then, Theo was, we were shouting, "come on, man, come on…"' His words tumbled from his lips. 'Quentin was ahead of me. Then a blast, God knows where from – you never get used to it, the smell, the ringing in your ears, just smoke, rain, head spinning, fear twisting your guts. I couldn't see him. Theo … I didn't know what I was doing, but I ran back, Quentin was shouting at me to get the hell out, but something made me …' He raised his head, but his eyes were empty, his sight elsewhere. 'He was dying. No leg … no … anything.' He took a breath, a shudder. 'Don't know how long I was there. Quentin dragged me away. "We must bury him," I was saying. "We must bury him." I kept saying it. Quentin said I was saying it all night, over and over again. I wake up saying it, even now …' He threw her a thin smile, as if unsure who she was.

126

'You loved him?'

'We loved each other. Like brothers. Theo, Quentin and me. Inseparable.'

The distant sea murmured in the silence. On the terraces the seagulls swooped and chirped.

'You are not guilty,' Agatha said to him.

He pitched himself towards her, grabbed her wrists in a tight grip. 'Mrs. Christie – I have no memory of it. Early Monday morning. I know nothing … I remember being on the tennis court. I remember seeing him lying there, the blood … I looked at my hand and there it was, the pistol, clutched between fingers which I knew to be mine but which I couldn't feel. I dropped the gun. I believe I shouted, called out. The staff found me there. Young Hughes, I remember … he took my arm, he led me away. I think it was him. Then I came to my senses. After that, I kept out of the way. Saw the police arrive, kept my distance.' Again, the mirthless smile.

'Mr. Farrar –'

'What? You think I should confess? You think I should just come clean?'

'Mr. Farrar – what is there to confess?'

His gaze now was clear. 'You and I, Mrs. Christie – we both have a fair idea who killed Mr. Collyer.' He got to his feet and stumbled from the room.

Chapter Twelve

Agatha sat, yawning, at her breakfast table. Saturday morning, she thought. She imagined Archie, too, sitting alone over breakfast, pouring his own tea, stirring in sugar, two spoons rather than the one she would allow him.

She found her attention drawn once more to the tennis party. She watched Blanche's edginess, the fretful way she made sure Kurt had bread rolls, butter, marmalade ... She thought about Blanche's words, about having to keep an eye on Mr. Farrar. It was perfectly clear, now, that Kurt himself must have initiated the whole trip, and that Blanche had been prevailed upon to look after him. She wondered what her husband made of these events, that an attempt to protect his dear friend had unexpectedly landed him at the centre of a murder scene.

'Oh dear, the staff do so insist I shouldn't sit alone ...' Nora was standing by her table. 'Even though I'm really quite happy with my own company. It turns out.'

Agatha smiled up at her, indicated the second chair, and Nora sat down.

'I mean,' Nora went on, 'who'd have thought that it would take these terrible events to show me that, actually, I'm not the shy, mousy girl I thought I was.'

Agatha poured her some tea. She noticed how the pinched, pale look had gone. The woman who sat opposite her was fresh-faced and smiling, her hair neatly pinned up, a simple silver string at her neck.

'Last night,' Nora went on, 'I stayed up late. I was reading a novel. Somerset Maugham, do you know him? I had no idea –' Her eyes were shining, her face animated. 'I had no idea,' she continued, 'that it could be like that, that you could open the pages of a book and be transported into a completely different world. China,' she exclaimed. 'And that poor woman, and the man she marries, and it's so sad, so terribly, terribly sad …' She looked across at Agatha. 'But it's not only sad. There's hope,' she said. 'You know at the end that things might be all right after all. I closed the book, and I looked out across the bay, with the moon across the sea, it was so late, the middle of the night, everything was quiet … and I thought, things might be all right after all.'

She took a sip of tea.

They do that, books, Agatha wanted to say. Restore order. Put things right. But the appropriate phrase wouldn't come, and she said nothing. After a moment, Nora spoke again.

'My mother, you see,' she said. 'In the novel, Kitty has to learn that she's not the shallow, silly girl that she's been brought up to be. And I looked at the moonlight on the still calm sea and I thought about my mother. And how her constant disapproval really didn't fit me for life at all. Just like Kitty. And the funny thing is –' Her eyes were bright as they fixed on Agatha – 'the funny thing is, Frederick didn't approve of novels. He wouldn't let me read them. This one happened to be on the shelves in my room here. If Frederick had been there, I'd never have dreamt of picking it up. And yet ...' She gave a sigh of happiness. 'Who'd have thought?' she said.

Nora reached for a slice of toast, then went on. 'Gossip, that's what Frederick called it. Pointless gossip, he'd say, when people talked about fiction. Last week, when Mr. Tyndall was telling me all about these papers of Dr. Adler's, and how worried he was about them coming to light, and asking me what Frederick was going to do with all that information, I really couldn't help him. I had no idea. So I just told him, that Frederick wasn't interested in gossip, and if there were secrets up at Langlands, which clearly, it turns out, there were, Frederick probably wouldn't even know about them. Chemistry, that's what he was writing about. That's what he'd say. "The work done by chemists is of the utmost importance," he'd always say. "If the general public comes to understand something of the contribution made by chemists, then my job will be done." I can't help thinking that Mr. Tyndall was worrying unnecessarily, going on about the artworks being shipped over from Moscow ...'

'Artworks from Russia?' Agatha tried not to stare at her.

'The poor man was so terribly anxious about it, Mr. Tyndall was. He wanted to know if Frederick had come upon Dr. Adler's intentions about the paintings. I had to say, I can't imagine my husband had any interest in paintings being donated to the Bolsheviks, or indeed, shipped back to the Cornish coast in the middle of the night. If you knew Frederick, I said to him ...' She waved her hand airily.

Agatha passed her the butter, and she began to spread some on her toast. 'Anyway,' she said, 'now I know about novels and how wonderful they are, I'm going to read and read and read. My brother's friend James, he said I'd enjoy a writer called Edith Wharton. American, apparently. He once promised to lend me one, it won a prize, apparently, he said it was awfully good. Of course, with Frederick there, I couldn't possibly have agreed, but now – oh good, here comes Oliver with my eggs. Mr. Finch brought him back from Langlands this morning, he said he was worried about the atmosphere there being bad for him, and I can't help but think he's right. Thank you dear,' she said, as Oliver served her two perfect fried eggs. 'Just how I like them.'

They finished their breakfast, Agatha and Mrs. Collyer, with some further discussion about novels, about whether they should always have a happy ending, about whether they should be true to real life or an escape from it.

'Oh, no,' Nora said, 'not an escape. An enhancement. You should be able to close the pages of a book and be that little bit wiser about life. That's what I think anyway. It's been so lovely talking to you, Mrs. Christie.' She gathered up her little clutch bag and glided away.

Agatha found her gaze drawn again to Kurt's table. An idea was forming, as she watched Blanche's nervous concern for her husband's friend, as Sebastian tried to talk to Sophie about her backhand, as Sophie, instead, waved at Oliver. Oliver waved back, with a large tray of empty plates wobbling on his other hand.

After breakfast, Agatha went to Mr. Finch's little office.

'Ah –' Finch looked up from his desk, from what appeared to be a pile of invoices. 'Mrs. Christie. The police appear to be making progress. I do hope you won't be imprisoned with us for much longer.'

'Mr. Finch.' She smiled. 'I'd hardly refer to your hotel as prison. I just wondered if I could enlist your help?'

'Of course, Madam, of course.'

'Mr. Farrar,' she said. 'He says he's stayed here before?'

Finch nodded.

'On just the one occasion?'

Finch frowned. 'I think so, yes. Last year.'

'Would you be able to show me when?'

'Of course.' He bent to a drawer, and pulled out a fat, foolscap, leather-bound book. 'This contains all the secrets of this place,' he smiled. 'My ledger,' he said. He began to leaf through it. 'Yes,' he said. 'Mr. Farrar came this time last year. I'm not aware of having encountered him before that.'

'Was he with Mrs. Winters?'

Finch looked thoughtful. He shook his head. 'No,' he said. 'The previous time he was alone. Ah, here we are. Yes, last May he was here for three days. I'm sure that was his first visit with us. I'd have noted his preferences, had I met him previously.'

'Do you remember much about him on this former occasion?'

Finch leaned back in his chair. He rubbed his chin. 'I can't say I do. I tend to leave my guests to their own devices.'

'And was Mr. Tyndall here too?'

132

He gave a nod. 'Mr. Tyndall is almost permanently a resident, and certainly, he was with us last year.' His brow furrowed, then he looked at her. 'I suppose it's true, now I come to think of it …' He met her eyes, as if an idea was dawning on him. 'But really, they had very little to do with one another. They don't give the impression of being closely acquainted, do they? In fact, if anything, they seem rather at daggers drawn.' He closed the book with a thud, looked at her again. 'What I don't like about this terrible business, Mrs. Christie, what I don't like at all, is how it has forced me to relinquish my professional principles. I've had to tell the police snippets of information about my guests. It's a breach of all my professional codes. I take these things very seriously.'

'You must know all the people involved,' Agatha said. 'The big house, the Adlers. Mr. Collyer's book, all this concern about the papers …'

A shadow crossed his face. 'That in particular. When Detective Inspector Olds was asking me about that dratted book, and I found myself describing the conversation I'd had with Mr. Tyndall …' He looked up at her with a look of pleading in his eyes. 'I really felt it was a breach of confidence. And what could I tell the poor man? I know nothing about Mr. Collyer's book, nothing at all. I'm only a hotel manager. And a soldier,' he added. 'Really, I know so little. I can't imagine I've been any help to the police at all.' His fingers twisted together in his lap. 'I'm only a squaddie, at heart.'

'I must be very difficult for you,' Agatha said. 'But at least young Oliver Hughes is back with us.'

He gave a warm smile. 'Frau Adler's care for Oliver has been such a comfort to us all, but after the police were there, yesterday, we felt he'd be safer getting on with his work here with me.'

Above him hung the painting. A strip of sunlight caught the edge of it. The frame glowed gold; the mother's face shone in the warm light.

Agatha turned once more to the manager. 'Mr. Finch, you've been so helpful. I have one other question.'

He gave a flinch of weariness, waited for her to speak.

'Do you think Mr. Farrar's previous visit coincided with the Collyers?' she asked.

He frowned, thought for a moment, then his expression cleared. 'Good heavens,' he said. He grabbed his books, flicked through the pages. 'Why, I do believe you're right. This time last year ...' His fingers raced through the leaves of paper. 'Here we are ...' He jabbed his finger at a line of neat black ink handwriting. 'You're absolutely right, Mrs. Christie. The Collyers were here for three weeks. But Mr. Farrar's three days coincided with the middle of their stay.'

Agatha took out her notebook, and copied down the dates. 'You've been very helpful,' she said. She stood up to go, and he got to his feet and followed her out to the corridor. His gaze went to the breakfast room, where Nora was still sitting, alone.

'Mrs. Collyer,' he said. 'I do wish the police would let her go. She can't be any further use to their investigation. And – oh dear – if you'll excuse me – they've served her marmalade, and I know she prefers jam.' With a small bow, he left Agatha's side and hurried into the breakfast room.

Agatha watched as he slipped to Nora's side, as he brought her a dish of raspberry jam. She saw her quiet smile of pleasure. She reflected on the change in Nora Collyer, this new blossoming of life in the wake of tragedy. 'Who'd have a thought a mere story could do that?' Nora had asked at breakfast.

A mere story, Agatha thought. Captain Wingfield was waiting by the old grey sundial. It was time that Martha Hobbes joined him there, to declare their love, to embark on their new life together.

Soon, she thought, I will write those pages. But first, she said to herself, heading along the hall towards the heavy front door, there is work to be done.

*

The sea was turquoise blue, sparkling with sunlight. The coastal track was dusted with sand. The air around her chirped with birdsong and the call of crickets. Ahead of her lay the village, the *Lady Leona* now almost entirely stripped of everything, the villagers no doubt poring over the empty metal crate. She wondered what had happened to the promise of gold.

She descended the path towards the ship.

Ghosts, she thought. The ghostly young woman waiting for her sailor to return. "The tide flows in, the tide flows out, twice every day returning…" The notes rang faintly in her mind.

She thought about the derelict house, Ince Hall. Theodore Munro's house, drifting with memories, echoing with the dead. She thought

135

about the three men, all artists, all devoted to each other. And only two came back.

'We loved each other,' Kurt said to her.

Love, she thought.

In her mind, she saw the old stone sundial of her story. In her mind, she saw James, whoever he was, offering the newly awoken Nora Collyer novels to read. An image, too, of Robin Tyndall and Frau Adler, the glances flickering between them, heavy with feeling. An image of the golf course, back home, of Archie, standing on the green. She imagined him, gazing out towards the chestnut trees with that vacant, distracted look he'd acquired since the war. She imagined him thinking of her, looking forward to her return.

Love, she thought. Perhaps all stories are about love.

She turned and descended the last few steps towards the beach.

'I'm afraid it's a disappointing outcome.' Bosun Walker was standing at the foot of the steps. He waved towards the ragged frame of the old ship. 'That metal box was indeed completely empty,' he said. 'Whatever secrets our ship here held went down with her. The villagers are still scavenging what they can, but I hold out little hope of anything of meaning. As Reggie Olds was saying earlier today, people will insist on clinging to their false hopes with these things. He said he blames the war. Everyone wants a story of redemption. Those poor men, those lives lost … people want to think it mustn't be in vain.' His gaze had travelled to the carcass of the ship, and his eyes seemed to cloud briefly with sadness. 'Mind you …' he turned back to her, all bluff good humour once more. 'Reggie Olds has got his own story to sew up, hasn't he just, with all these goings-on at the hotel.' He began to lead the way, towards the shipwreck. She fell into step with him, following him across the shingle. Seagulls dipped and swerved overhead.

'And as for that empty crate,' he said. 'We'll never know about that one, I reckon. A closed book.' They skirted the side of the ship, the holes open in her bow. 'Odd thing, last night,' he said, 'We had help. Chap from the big house, don't suppose you know him? Olds says he's the secretary up there. Dark haired, artistic sort of chap. He was here. Carrying planks, along with that other man, friend of the lady up there at the big house.'

'Robin Tyndall?' Agatha said.

A nod from the Bosun. 'Aye, that's the one. Couldn't be more helpful. You've seen the weight of those things. Ferrying them to and fro for us, they were. One thin as a rake, the other with a gammy leg, but they worked as hard as any of my men.' They were on the wet sand now, and he turned and surveyed the ship. The edges of the waves lapped against the wreckage in melancholy companionship.

'It was as if they'd come for some other reason,' the Bosun was saying. 'That's what I said to Reggie Olds. As if it were a cover for some other purpose.'

Agatha watched a seagull perch on the broken mast.

'Funny thing, see,' Ted Walker went on. 'They've been here before, the people from the big house. The woman from there. And then, last week, there he was, alone, the man with the stick, standing, waiting for a ship. One of my boys here saw him too. But no ship

137

arrived. Standing there at dawn, and then heading back to the hotel where he chooses to spend his days.' He gave a shrug. 'Oh well. Funny old world. Not for me to question what folks get up to.'

They began to walk away from the ship, away from the encroaching tide.

'So you told Inspector Olds about Mr. Tyndall being here?'

'Oh, aye.' The Bosun took out his pipe, considered it between his fingers. 'It made quite an impression on him. He pinned the boy down, too, wanted to know which day it was. Sunday night, it was, small hours of Monday morning. And then Reggie Olds, gives a little jump of joy. "Ha!" he said. Said it was the last bit of the jigsaw. Heaven knows what he meant by that. But I tell you, all the time I've known Reggie Olds, I've never known him make a mistake. Mind you ...' He took a pinch of tobacco from the pouch at his belt, tapped it into the bowl of his pipe. '... this case is far bigger than anything else he's known. The only time we've had anything like this, it was back before the war, the old pharmacist down by Fowey caught poisoning his wife. But Olds brought the villain to justice then, and I don't see any reason to suppose he won't bring this chap to justice just the same.'

They began to walk up the path, past the ruined cottage. He jabbed his pipe towards the thick cracked glass of the windows. 'Shame we can't ask her,' he said, with a smile. 'Young Tilly, our ghost here, she sees all the comings and goings along this coast. Waiting here, mourning for her sailor-boy. The story goes that he went out with a crew carrying tea across to Italy. He promised her a fine pair of shoes on his return. "A fine pair of leather shoes, fit for a lady," the story goes. And he never came back. And that's why, they reckon, whenever she's been sighted, she's barefoot. Some have her in her plain wooden clogs, waiting for her fine Venetian shoes.' He shrugged. 'That's the story. For those that believe in ghosts.'

'And do you, Bosun?'

He stopped, his gaze settled on the ruined cottage.

'What I think is, people need their stories. But no.' He shook his head. 'I think the dead are gone from here. No need for them to stay.' He looked as if he might say more, but instead he gave a smile, doffed his hat. 'Well, I bid you a good morning. If I were you, I'd get back to the hotel. Reggie Olds seems to think he'll be making an arrest later on today.'

With a rough squeeze of her hand, he was gone. She watched him make his way back to the listing hulk, watched him issue orders, watched the villagers scurry at his word.

Chapter Thirteen

She turned away, began to ascend the hill, past the village. The sea whispered softly. Sunshine flickered on white-painted walls.

So, she thought, an arrest is about to be made. The killer of Mr. Collyer is about to be unmasked.

She wondered how Inspector Olds could be so sure.

The sun beat down, as she reached the summit. The path forked, with one track continuing along the coast towards the hotel. The other path led away from the coast, and she recognized the copse of trees, behind which hid the ruin of Ince Hall. On an impulse, she turned and followed the path, appreciating the cool shade of the pine branches overhead.

The door creaked on its half-rusted hinges. She pushed it open, found herself inside. It seemed different, now she was alone, now she wasn't seeing it through Kurt's eyes. She noticed new details; a rough-hewn alcove in which was carved a small stone image, Our Lady, Agatha thought, as she gazed at the veiled figure. The woman's eyes gazed upwards in adoration, her hands clasped in intercession.

Built by Catholics, Kurt had said, centuries ago. It certainly feels deserted, Agatha thought, as she wandered through the rooms. It seemed chillier, creakier. At her feet, dry leaves flicked and circled in the draught. She crossed the hall, walked down the passageway, came out into the studio where Kurt had taken her before.

The studio, too, seemed darker now, without his presence. 'Ghosts,' he'd said, as if he'd made the room come alive, with his memories of the artists gathered there, their talents being pooled to help the war effort.

Camouflage, she thought. Mimicry or disguise. She traced her finger along the peeling wallpaper, the sooty outlines where the paintings had hung.

The war broke all the rules.

She stood in the middle of the room, listening to the rustle of the mice, and wondered why she'd come.

In the empty fireplace she could see three stacked frames, wooden-crated paintings, she realized, as she approached them. Clean, dustless – clearly only recently placed here, she thought. Certainly, they weren't here before.

She knelt down, peered inside the crating, tried to see the artwork within. Between the slats of packing, she could make out soft grey brush-strokes, an outline of a man in soldier's uniform.

She got to her feet, dusted cobwebs from her skirt.

Bosun Walker's words came to her, about the secretary from the big house being so helpful with the shipwreck. About Mr. Tyndall being sighted on the beach at night, waiting, 'as if for a ship to come in.'

Sunday night, the Bosun had said. And Mr. Collyer was found dead early Monday morning.

And in the meantime, three paintings have appeared in this house.

She left the studio, made her way back into the hall. She stood where Kurt had stood, in front of the dusty square, where the Antigone painting had hung.

'As Hades and the dead are witnesses …' The words seemed to whisper in the air around her.

In her mind, she saw the absent painting. The three figures, anguished in love, united in death. The brother's corpse, the sister prepared to sacrifice so much; her lover, pleading with her to come away.

How heavy war still weighs, she thought. How constant are the battles we still fight.

The empty square stared back at her.

Mimicry. And disguise.

Reluctantly, she turned away, made her way to the front door. The figure of Our Lady sat neatly, benignly, in her alcove. Agatha paused in front of her, and the statue returned her gaze with a look of infinite understanding.

The Mother of God, Agatha thought.

Detective Inspector Olds is right, she thought. It is time to make an arrest.

She left the house, latching the crooked front door behind her as best she could.

She hurried back up the path, strode along the coastal track and arrived, breathless, at the hotel.

She was met by young Hughes. 'Mrs. Christie – they've been looking for you,' he said. 'I was sent to find you. The police are here.' A shadow of anxiety crossed his face. 'I don't like it, Ma'am, I really don't.'

She placed a hand on his shoulder. 'There's nothing to worry about,' she said. 'I am sure justice is about to be done.'

'You are?' He looked up at her, with his wide brown eyes.

She smiled at him. 'I am,' she said. 'In fact, I have one question for you, if you don't mind.'

'Of course, Ma'am.'

They were standing at the side of the entrance steps.

'On Monday morning, Master Hughes, you were already up.'

He nodded, uncertainly.

'You were first on the scene?'

Another nod. He was chewing his lip.

'And you saw Mr. Collyer, lying there.'

He gave a shudder.

'And Mr. Farrar standing over him?'

'Yes, Ma'am.'

'Can you describe what you saw?'

'Oh, Mrs. Christie,' he burst out. 'It was horrid. So horrid. Mr. Finch took me away as soon as he could, but I saw him, Mr. Collyer, and there was a noise he was making, such a horrid, horrid noise. And then it stopped. And Mr. Farrar was standing there, staring at the body on the ground. And when I got there he looked at me, Mr.

143

Farrar did, holding the gun, and it was like he didn't see me. And he kept saying the same thing, over and over.'

'And what was he saying?'

'He was saying, "we must bury him." He kept saying it, over and over, "we must bury him …" And then it was like he saw I was there, and he looked down, and dropped the gun, and then he just ran, ran away … Then Mr. Finch came and hurried me away, didn't want me seeing such things he said.'

'Did you see Mr. Tyndall, by any chance?'

The boy's face clouded. He gave a nod. 'I remember thinking, what's the gentlemen doing up so early. I told Mr. Finch I'd seen him there, and he agreed it was strange. Very strange.'

'What was he doing, Mr. Tyndall?'

Again, the troubled frown. 'He was just standing, over by the old oak tree.'

'Do you think he could see Mr. Farrar?'

'He was looking that way, yes.'

'And he was dressed, you say?'

Another nod. 'His jacket, and hat, Mrs. Christie. He always wears them.'

'Did you tell the police, Master Hughes?'

He nodded. 'Oh, yes, Ma'am. Mr. Finch said we must make sure that we tell the Inspector, so we did.'

She patted his shoulder. 'Good,' she said. 'And now you must put it all behind you.'

'That's what Frau Adler said too. Everyone has been so good to me, Mrs. Christie.'

'Hah!' came a familiar voice. Agatha turned to see Mr. Farrar approaching the steps, as Oliver slipped away towards the kitchen garden.

'And so we go in,' Mr. Farrar said. He took a last inhale of his cigarette, stubbed it out on the stone balustrade. 'I had considered fleeing, again,' he said. 'But then I thought, for all these years I have been on the run. And now, it is time to stop.' He threw her a clear, grey look. 'Last night I didn't sleep. I sat outside, here –' he waved his arm towards the hotel gardens – 'and I reflected upon it. All of it. I asked myself, what is life for? Because I have to admit, Mrs. Christie, that for some time it has seemed without meaning.'

'And what did you conclude?'

He looked at her. He was crisply dressed and sober. 'I concluded that the point of life is to punch you about so much that in the end you don't fear death.' There was a taut, bleak nervousness about him. 'In brief, I realized that it was time to stop running away,' he said, with an empty smile. 'Look, here they all are.' He pointed at the hotel's front door.

There were cars parked outside the hotel entrance. The old police Austin. The sleek Buick from the big house. Agatha felt Kurt tense at the sight of the cars. 'Thus I meet my destiny,' he said, quietly.

Holding open the door of the Buick stood Robin Tyndall. He too looked anxious, waiting stiffly as Lillian Adler unfurled herself from the car, as Quentin Fitzwilliam followed her into the hotel.

Kurt had taken Agatha's arm, more for his support than hers, she realized. His grip as he leaned on her tightened, as they made their way inside.

Chapter Fourteen

They gathered in the Palm Court. The staff were assembled too, all in white, standing to attention by the baize door. Robin Tyndall pulled out a chair for Lilian Adler, then settled himself beside her, Quentin on the other side. Blanche and Sophie were already seated, with Sebastian in attendance, as ever, and Kurt relinquished his grip of Agatha's arm and stumbled towards them, threw himself into a chair at their table.

Nora sat alone, a novel in her hands, her attention completely absorbed in its pages. The shrill Scottish ladies were nowhere to be seen.

Agatha took a table at one side. Inspector Olds and Sergeant Brierley were also seated, and now the Inspector got to his feet, cleared his throat, Sergeant Brierley picked up his notebook, and a hush settled on the room. Young Oliver was standing with the staff, and Finch stood protectively at his side.

Inspector Olds began to describe the day of the killing, how it was at about six in the morning, how a gunshot was heard, how poor Mr. Collyer was found in the throes of death from a single bullet wound fired at close range, how Mr. Farrar was the only one on the courts and found with the body. He talked about how the day before, Mr. Collyer had arranged to have a tennis lesson with Mr. Farrar. He said that Mr. Travers, here, a qualified tennis coach had offered, but that

Mr. Collyer, for some reason, had accepted Mr. Farrar's offer instead. The Inspector went on to explain how Frau Adler, too, had arrived on the scene, having been driven to the hotel early by her secretary, Mr. Fitzwilliam, because of her anxiety about the papers that Mr. Collyer had acquired for his biographical work.

Inspector Olds' gaze settled on Mr. Farrar, as he explained that Mr. Farrar had admitted that he'd arranged the tennis game because he knew that Mr. Collyer had acquired papers relating to a group of painters, of which Mr. Farrar was a part. An event had taken place during the war, the details of which Mr. Farrar did not want revealed.

Inspector Olds took a deep breath. 'All we need now, is to show that it was you, Mr. Farrar, who wielded that pistol. Who'd lured poor Mr. Collyer to the tennis courts, and who now, in the hope of hiding his secrets once and for all, was prepared to kill. And,' Inspector Olds went on, 'I would say, that we have that proof.'

'The pistol –' Kurt's voice as he interrupted was almost a shout. 'You tell me,' he said. 'How did I get the pistol from Mr. Finch's office on to the courts? I have no idea, myself, no memory of it at all …'

Blanche placed a calming hand on his arm. Kurt quietened, shaking his head.

'There's more,' Inspector Olds continued. 'Mr. Tyndall …' He turned to him. 'You, too, were not far from the tennis courts at the moment of these unfortunate events, were you not?'

Mr. Tyndall stared at the Inspector. He seemed about to speak, but said nothing.

'I put it to you,' Inspector Olds continued, 'that you hadn't been to bed at all. That you'd been waiting on the shore, for a ship to come in.'

Robin Tyndall's voice was tight. 'That is in fact the case, Inspector. But it has nothing to do with the death of Mr. Collyer.'

'Oh, it doesn't, does it?' Reginald Olds began to pace the room, his thumbs tucked into his waistcoat pockets. 'Even given the fact that Mr. Collyer's researches had got too close for comfort?'

Tyndall's gaze was fixed on the floor in front of him.

The Inspector addressed the room. 'I may be a mere police officer, but I have the very great advantage of having lived in these parts all my life. And when it comes to nailing the facts of the case, this gives me what one might call the trump card. My Sergeant here will support me in this.' He glanced at Brierley, who gave an obedient nod of agreement. 'This shore line,' the Inspector went on, 'is like a second home to me. All its caves, and beaches, all its nooks and crannies, I've known them since childhood. And not just the places, but the people too. So, when Bosun Walker sees something he thinks I should know, he tells me.'

Kurt was sitting, upright, calmer now, Blanche close at his side. Both had their eyes fixed on the policeman.

'And what the Bosun had to tell me is of great relevance to the death of poor Mr. Collyer,' the Inspector said.

Nora Collyer, too, was still and attentive, her book closed in her lap. She gave a small wince at her husband's name.

'Ted Walker had noticed various comings and goings at night, over the last couple of weeks,' Reginald Olds was saying. 'People waiting for ships, odd lights being shone out to sea as if to give a signal.' He paused, surveyed the room, the collection of faces all turned towards him. 'And it is true to say, that our investigation has unearthed quite a chain of events. What started as the death of one unfortunate individual, has, shall we say, blossomed into quite a story. It's a story that extends all the way to those Russian Bolshies, but has its heart right here amongst us. Yes, even here, in the quiet beauty of our Cornish coast, it turns out there are people with sympathies for the Soviet revolutionaries. I shall be making a report to my superiors in London on just this subject. As the Home Secretary himself has said, in these times where revolution is in the air, we must stop at nothing to prevent it taking hold.'

His voice was loud. He allowed his gaze to alight on the assembled company, then continued, in a slightly softer tone. 'Our investigations into the shipping of Bolshevik contraband will continue at the highest level. However, as a police officer, I owe it to my men to make sure that I consider the facts as they are in this case. So, ladies and gentlemen, let us return to the facts surrounding the death of Mr. Collyer. And the facts are these. Firstly, only one shot was fired. From only one pistol. Secondly, only one person was actually present at the moment of the death of Mr. Collyer. And thirdly, that person, who was present, had every reason to wish to silence Mr. Collyer. For it is the case, ladies and gentlemen, that Mr. Collyer's pioneering researches into Dr. Adler had brought him directly into danger from two different sources, in a way that he couldn't possibly have predicted.'

Agatha glanced at Nora. Nora was staring at the policeman with a look of incomprehension, a small frown on her pretty face, as she tried to match the leaden writings of her dull chemist husband with this picture of daring scholarship.

The policeman continued, 'I have always said, that I stick with the facts. And in these modern times, we are aided in our quest by scientific methods. We now have the results back from the fingerprint matching of the murder weapon. And the facts, ladies and gentlemen, are these. That of the two sets of fingerprints found on the weapon, one belong to those of its owner, and the other – to Mr. Farrar.' He waited for the effect of this statement to sink in.

'And so,' the Inspector continued, 'we come to our conclusion. The facts are as I have outlined. Which means, that we only have one possible outcome. Which is to charge you, Mr. Farrar, with the murder of Mr. Frederick Collyer.'

Everyone turned to look at Kurt Farrar, then back at the Inspector, who stood tall in the middle of the room, his sergeant by his side.

But now Kurt jumped to his feet. 'You can't!' Kurt shouted. 'I didn't … I had no reason …' His fists were clenched, his breathing loud. Blanche reached out but he sidestepped her grasp, still shouting incoherently. Blanche then turned to Agatha, with a look of burning pleading in her eyes.

Agatha took a deep breath, smoothed her hair, and got to her feet. 'Detective Inspector,' she said, and her voice seemed to settle the room. Kurt looked across at her, limped back to his chair, folded himself back on to it. Blanche put her hand on his arm once more.

Agatha faced the police team. 'There's one part of the story that is missing,' she said.

The Inspector looked at her. 'Mrs. Christie,' he began. 'I cannot imagine there is.'

'Detective Inspector,' she repeated, trying to keep her voice steady. 'Perhaps I might just explain.'

He tapped his fingers on his waistcoat pocket. He glanced around the room.

'It won't take long,' she said.

He gave a reluctant nod of acquiescence.

She smoothed her skirt, settled her breathing. 'So,' she said. 'As you say, it's about ten to six in the morning, and Frederick Collyer has been called to the tennis court, by Mr. Farrar here. He's expecting a game of tennis, as he wants to improve, and Mr. Farrar has offered to help. As you also say, Mr. Travers had already offered, but Mr. Farrar stepped in, rather oddly, as you've pointed out. But Mr. Collyer, with all due respect, had already made rather clear his view that Mr. Farrar was a better player than Mr. Travers.'

She glanced at Sebastian, who gave his shiny, tennis-coach smile.

She went on, 'Now, what we know is, the revolver had been removed from Mr. Finch's office, early that morning, and was in fact right next to the tennis court, just lying there, loaded, by the nets.

Someone had planned this quite carefully, knowing that there would be a moment when there would be just the two of them on the tennis courts.'

'Well, of course, we know all this,' the Inspector said. 'Mr. Farrar did just that.' There was a tone of impatience in his voice. 'He'd got rid of the tennis coach, he'd arranged a match very early in the morning, and so, there he was, alone with Mr. Collyer.'

'That's possible, yes,' Agatha said. 'But, given how early it was, an awful lot of the guests were already up and dressed. Mr. Tyndall, for example, as you've pointed out.'

'We've dealt with Mr. Tyndall,' the Inspector said, testily.

'Yes,' Agatha agreed. She turned to face Mr. Tyndall. 'Bosun Walker says he'd seen you down on the coast, at first light that morning. He thought you were waiting for a ship to come in, but none did, and after a while you'd headed back to the hotel, he thought.'

Robin Tyndall faced her, silently. The Inspector was tapping his foot. 'We've established all this, Mrs. Christie. If you've nothing more to add –'

Agatha again addressed Mr. Tyndall. 'In fact, whatever the ship was that you were waiting for, seems to have come in last night. And three crated paintings were docked, and carried by you and Mr. Fitzwilliam up to the old house.'

'Tyndall!' The word was a loud shout, from Mr. Farrar. 'You got them? Last night? Why in heaven's name didn't you tell me?'

Mr. Tyndall turned, slowly, to face Mr. Farrar. 'Quentin wanted to tell you himself. I assume he hasn't yet done so.'

Mr. Farrar's expression settled, as he absorbed this information. He looked at Quentin Fitzwilliam, who was gazing straight at him but said nothing.

The Inspector broke the silence. 'Paintings?' he asked. He stared at Robin Tyndall, then at Quentin Fitzwilliam. Then he appeared to gather himself. 'But none of this,' he said, 'has the slightest bit to do with the death of Mr. Collyer. In the end, there was only one man on the tennis courts at the point of the poor man's murder, and I still maintain, that Mr. Farrar, in the end, was that man.'

'No,' Agatha said. 'Mr. Farrar couldn't be that man. Because Mr. Farrar was not present at the moment of the death of Mr Collyer. Were you?'

'Mr. Farrar has insisted he was indeed present when the terrible events unfolded,' the policeman spluttered.

Kurt was staring at Agatha, wide-eyed.

'I put it to you, Mr. Farrar,' she said, 'that you had only just arrived at the hotel. After the shot had been fired. Had any of the staff ventured to your room so early, I imagine they'd find your bed hadn't been slept in. The truth is, you had stayed at Langlands that night.'

There was a collective gasp followed by silence.

Agatha continued, 'At the moment you arrived back for your meeting with Frederick, which was nothing to do with improving his tennis, and everything to do with the biography of Dr. Adler and his

154

connection with your artist friends, you heard a shot. Just as you arrived. The sound triggered a kind of trauma in you.'

Kurt's gaze was unflinching, but his whole body seemed to tremble.

'That's why you were found, at the scene of the crime, apparently uttering words of guilt.'

Blanche Winters was staring at Kurt. Now her voice cut through the silence. 'Kurt – you slept at the house?'

He was staring straight ahead. He said nothing.

'Kurt – you'd promised.' Blanche's tone was distressed.

Kurt began to speak. His voice was an odd, blank monotone. 'I had to see him,' Kurt said. 'He was the only one who knew the truth. I'd forgotten the tennis game with Frederick, then remembered it just in time. Mrs. Christie is right.'

Quentin Fitzwilliam had taken a step towards him. 'Kurt,' he said. 'Where were you? Why didn't you come in?'

Kurt met his gaze. 'The rose garden,' he said. 'The bench there. Watching the moon ...'

'I was awake,' Quentin said. 'I had a feeling ...'

'I tried to pluck up courage ...'

'You should have come in.'

'I tried the front door. Once. About three in the morning ... It was bolted ...'

'I heard it,' Quentin said. 'I heard the latch lift ... I almost came downstairs to see. Thought perhaps I'd dreamt it ...'

The two men's eyes were locked. After a moment, Kurt turned back to Agatha. 'And then it was the dawn. And I was sitting, chilled to the bone, on that stone bench. And then I remembered the tennis game ... I got up and ran down to the hotel, got to my room, grabbed my tennis shoes and headed for the courts, just as – just as ...'

'You heard the shot,' Blanche said.

'I ran towards the noise. I found him. He was bleeding ... terrible noise of his breathing. I don't remember what I did ... must have picked up the gun ... the noise, the rattle of a dying man ... Dying ...' Kurt's words faded to an incoherent murmur then stopped. He stared emptily downwards.

The air settled around them. Inspector Olds looked at Sergeant Brierley, then at the floor.

'You've all been searching in the wrong place,' Agatha said. 'It turns out, this is a very simple story after all.' She crossed the room and took Nora by the hands. Nora looked up at her, with a smile of warmth and friendship.

'What people wish is for your happiness, Mrs. Collyer,' she said. 'And, without wishing to be indiscreet, your marriage was not always a source of happiness to you. You'd stayed here on three occasions, due to your husband's research at Langlands, and each time, the people who coincided with you witnessed your unhappiness, the crushing of your spirit, the efforts you made to please a man who was determined not to be pleased. More than that, they saw your maternal soul, your wistful sense of loss about your chance to be a mother. To see that die away, to see you lose that opportunity, for people who cared about you, it was too painful to witness. And after a while, a very clear plan was formulated. Simply, to liberate you from this misery.'

Nora was staring at her, uncomprehending.

'There was the fuss about the steak, that evening.' Agatha still faced her. 'Your husband's rough treatment of young Hughes. And then there was the pudding. All that trouble that someone had gone to, to make you happy. The strawberry meringue was the last straw, wasn't it? That's when the idea fixed itself in the mind of your husband's killer. Frederick had already made a plan to have a tennis lesson, very early the next morning. And then, Mr. Farrar's absence as the day dawned served the killer's purposes all too well. After that, it was just a matter of making sure we all got distracted by these tales from Langlands, of secret affairs, missing papers and Bolshevik contraband.'

Sergeant Brierley glanced at his boss, then put down his notebook with a defeated look.

Agatha let go of Nora's hands, and stood in the middle of the room. She looked around her, at all the expectant faces. 'This is indeed a story of camouflage,' Agatha said. 'It's a tale of the masking of the truth. One shot was fired at close range. That's all it took. And then, it occurred to our killer that all he needed to do was leave the murder weapon exactly where it was, with his fingerprints on it – given that it was his own pistol.'

The space shifted in the room. Around the table there were intakes of breath.

She turned to Mr. Finch. 'I couldn't understand why everyone was fighting over this biography. When I read those drafts, at last, and realized how dull it was, I began to see that it was a pretence. This morning you mentioned how you'd had to tell the police that Mr. Tyndall was asking about the papers. I wondered, why would Mr. Tyndall have come to you about the papers. Then I realized, that it must have been you who approached him – you must have laid the ground some days before, by deliberately telling Mr. Tyndall that Mr. Collyer was due to reveal certain truths. Firstly, about the true nature of his relationship with Frau Adler. And secondly, about the shipping of certain British paintings out to the Bolsheviks in Moscow, and subsequent attempts to get them back. At that point, Mr. Tyndall panicked, and told you, Frau Adler. And then you, Frau Adler, insisted on getting the papers back from Frederick. You came to the hotel specifically to do so. At the same time, Mr. Farrar, too, remembered his tennis lesson, and realized that his absence would be noticed. That is why everyone had gathered on the tennis courts so early on Monday morning.' She paused, walked over to the fireplace. 'As I say, this is a story of simplicity. Our murderer fired the shot, from behind, put the gun down and left the scene. Within seconds there were two people at the tennis courts – Mr. Collyer, who was breathing his last; and Mr. Farrar, who had run towards the sound of gunfire. And then, a few moments later, the staff arrived, the police were called, and we know the rest.'

She surveyed the room. 'As Mr. Farrar said to me before, there are two paths to hiding what one wants hidden – you either cover it, or you make it fit in with its surroundings. Concealment or mimicry. All Mr. Finch needed was an alibi, which young Oliver dutifully provided, as indeed, Mr. Finch was with him almost all the time. Almost. But when poor Oliver confessed that he'd been first at the scene, I realized there must have been a moment before that when, indeed, Mr. Finch could have been anywhere. And I believe that Mr. Finch realized that too, which is why he spirited Oliver away to Langlands for a few days, to get him out of the way and avoid any questions.'

Mr. Finch was staring fixedly at Agatha, stiff-backed and expressionless. Agatha glanced at him, then turned to Kurt. 'So, Mr. Farrar, you were on the tennis courts, holding the murder weapon. It was at that point that you realized how things looked. You began to say that you'd just appeared at the scene of the crime. But your main alibi was not one you wished to reveal, believing, as you did, that it would raise more questions than it answered.'

Sebastian was standing behind Blanche, his hands on her shoulders. Quentin was by the window, framed by sunlight. Lillian Adler was sitting upright and immobile, glancing from time to time at Mr. Tyndall.

Agatha turned back to Mr. Finch. 'In the end, this is a very simple story. And the true heartbreak of it, is that the very happiness you were trying to bring about is not a happiness that you will be able to share.'

Mr. Finch was standing, his hands gripped into fists at his sides, his eyes locked with Agatha's as he listened to her speech. When she had finished, he turned to look at Mrs. Collyer. His gaze settled on her for some moments, and his posture softened, his fingers uncurled, his shoulders relaxed. Then he turned back to Agatha, and gave a simple nod of his head.

Detective Inspector Olds took a step towards him, but Mr. Finch held up his hand, and began to speak.

'I acted only out of love,' Finch said. His gaze went once more to Nora. He spoke again, his eyes fixed on hers. 'And even now, I have no regrets. Even though I can never give you the happiness you deserve, Mrs. Collyer, at least now you will be free to find that happiness with someone. With a kind man, one who will give you the children you so crave. Nora, if I may …' His voice cracked as he uttered her name. He went on, 'I encountered you two years ago, when you first came here with your husband for his research. And then, again, last year, when once again you spent a few precious weeks in this establishment. I came to see things as they were, that a woman who should love music, art, literature, was being deprived of such things – that a woman who, it seemed to me, would be a wonderful mother, was being kept from such joy. As time wore on, I saw you begin to shrink, to shrivel, to atrophy. And it made my heart break. But now, you have a chance to live the life you should live. Now I shall think of you as the woman you really are, with a song on your lips, with the laughter of the young around you, a baby in your arms. Nora –' Again, the tightening of his voice at her name. 'Nora – I have no regrets.'

There was a long silence. Nora was looking up at him, her eyes filled with tears, her hair shining in the sunlight.

Detective Inspector Olds cleared his throat. 'Mr. Finch – are you saying – are you saying that you are single-handedly responsible for the death of Frederick Collyer?'

Mr. Finch stood proud, tall and soldierly. He faced the Inspector. 'All this time I watched that man destroy the happiness of his wife. And as time passed, I realized that I loved her. That she was a woman worthy of love. That she deserved better than that selfish bully that she'd had the ill fortune to marry. More than that,' he went on, 'I saw how virtuous she was, how hard she worked to make her husband content, how little he valued her efforts. Half the time he was too stupid even to notice them.' He turned to Agatha. 'As you so rightly say, Madam, it is a simple story. My mistake was in choosing to complicate it, by weaving a web of tales about Dr. Adler's papers and Bolshevik paintings. But I have no regrets. All I wanted, was that the woman I love should be free to find happiness. I hope that by my actions she now will be.' He turned to the policeman. 'You may arrest me now. As far as I'm concerned, justice has been done.'

He tipped his hand to his head in a military salute.

With an awkward step, the Inspector approached him. He rattled a pair of handcuffs from their leather pouch, reluctantly locked Mr. Finch's wrists, turned towards the door. The two of them walked from the room at a stately pace, followed by Sergeant Brierley, his head bowed.

There was silence in the lounge. Even the sea seemed to have retreated, to whisper to itself far away.

Kurt Farrar was sitting quite still, staring at the carpet at his feet. Quentin Fitzwilliam was by the door, gazing unmoving in his direction. Nora was weeping, silently, and now Lillian crossed the room to her and sat next to her, and put an arm around her shoulders. Mr. Tyndall sat on the other side of her, murmuring words of comfort.

It was Blanche who broke the silence. 'Well,' she said. 'Now we don't have Finch to organize tea for us, we'll just have to do it ourselves.'

She went to the baize door, and as she did so, Kurt lifted his head and looked across at Quentin Fitzwilliam. Quentin walked slowly towards him. Kurt got to his feet, and the two men embraced.

Chapter Fifteen

The three paintings were unpacked, leaning side by side against the sandstone fireplace. Agatha, Kurt and Quentin all stood in what had been the studio of Ince Hall, gazing at them. The works showed soldiers; ordinary men, Agatha saw, not the glory of the officer class but tin-hatted youths, angular against the grey and ochre backgrounds. She saw the soft muddied wash sliced sharp with rifle butts, the curl of barbed wire, the polished buttons of a uniform against a twisted corpse.

The room was chilled, despite the Saturday morning brightness outside.

Yesterday, Finch had declared his love for Nora Collyer. Yesterday, Finch had declared himself a soldier. Yesterday, he had been driven away by the police to the Camborne cells, awaiting trial.

The hotel had been frozen in shock, silent in absorbing the truths of the ending of the life of Mr. Frederick Collyer.

Now it was a bright Saturday morning, and Agatha had been brought back to Ince Hall by Kurt and Quentin. Quentin had fetched them from the hotel. The three of them had sat silent in the Buick, no longer the tight, fearful silence of the last few days, but now a gentle, reflective calm, the sea a stretch of blue at their side along the coast, until they'd turned off and the car had crunched up the drive and come to a halt by the still-grand front steps.

Now the two men stood, gazing at the paintings. Kurt was still, his gaze fixed on the images. Quentin was by the window, half-leaning on the rotting frame.

Kurt shifted, breathed out. 'Theodore,' he said. 'What a painter the man was. What an artist.' He turned away from the paintings to face Quentin. 'You landed all these?' he said.

'Thursday night,' Quentin said.

'With Tyndall?'

Quentin nodded. 'I wanted to tell you,' Quentin said. 'I was so longing for you to be part of it all.'

Kurt stared at the old parquet of the floor, tapping at a leaf with the toe of his shoe.

'You were so far away,' Quentin said. 'And with images like this … I didn't want to add to what was already in your mind.'

Kurt raised his eyes, turned towards Agatha. 'I'd be even further away if it wasn't for this lady here.'

Agatha smiled, shook her head.

'I was lost,' Kurt went on. 'Lost. All I could remember is looking down at that man on the tennis court, seeing the blood, hearing the rattle of his breath. And then in my hand, the pistol, just grasped between my fingers, as if it all belonged to someone else … And then, yesterday, with the police there, telling me that all the facts showed that I was the only person who could have shot him…' His words faded to silence.

Quentin approached the fireplace. He touched the frame of one of the paintings. 'Facts,' he said. 'They only get us so far.'

Both men studied the images again. Then Kurt turned to Quentin. 'Theo,' he said. He drew a finger along one of the paintings. 'To think he came home after all.'

'Robin was dubious,' Quentin said. 'He said, what if it was Theo's wish that his work should belong to the comrades. But I said, what about this place? What about this beautiful house? At least until we sort out Theo's house, at least let's celebrate his work.'

'What did he say, Tyndall?' Kurt leaned against the peeling wallpaper.

'He came round in the end. Then it was a matter of persuading Lillian to go against her husband's wishes. Her argument, too, was that Theodore would have wanted the Soviets to have them, and that therefore Ernest would have supported him, and she didn't want to go against her husband's views after his death.' Quentin strolled across the room, flicked at the cobwebs on the mantelpiece. 'And of course, Robin's position is somewhat delicate. Frau Adler is poised between her husband and her lover in these things.'

'But she listened to you.' Kurt rested his hand briefly on Quentin's arm.

Quentin looked at him. 'Yes,' he said, after a moment. 'I suppose she did. I think, in the end, they could both see I was right.'

'What will happen to this house?'

Quentin surveyed the space around him. 'We're fighting to allow it to be kept in trust. As you know, he left no will. There's a cousin, a much older woman, she lives in Guildford, married to a solicitor. But they don't really want the bother. I think if we can set up the trust and keep Theo's family name, I think they'll be content with that in the end. And then this place can be restored, and looked after.'

Kurt went over to the paintings. He stood, stooped, breathless, in front of them. 'Theo,' he murmured. 'If only we could have saved you.'

Quentin was at his side.

'I loved him,' Kurt said.

'We both loved him,' Quentin said.

'I needed to bury him ...' Kurt's words hung in the air. He turned to Quentin. 'You say there's a grave now ...?'

Quentin nodded. 'We'll visit, Kurt. We'll pay our respects.'

Kurt reached out and touched one of the paintings. He traced the lines of the soldier's face. 'Yes,' he said. 'We'll do that. No more running away.'

'You had your reasons,' Quentin said. His gaze went once more to the soldier in the painting, the detail of the fingers twisted round the rifle. 'It's the problem with the fighting of battles,' he said. 'Sometimes it's difficult to know when to stop.'

Kurt met his eyes, threw him a small smile. 'Yes,' he said. 'But perhaps now ... perhaps now the battle is over.' He turned to Agatha. 'I owe you a huge debt of gratitude. We both do.'

'I just did what I could,' Agatha said.

'Camouflage,' he said. 'You were absolutely right. The butler camouflaged his own actions too – another layer of concealment.'

'He's not a butler,' Agatha said.

Kurt laughed, and Quentin laughed too, and the space around them seemed to breathe. 'We should get back,' Kurt said. 'Everyone's packing their bags to leave. You too, Mrs. Christie.'

'Yes,' she said. 'I'm on the morning train to London first thing tomorrow.'

They made their way towards the hall. 'Your husband will be delighted, I imagine,' Kurt said. 'All set to run along the platform at Paddington station to take you in his arms. Just like in your story.'

Agatha smiled, but her mind snagged against the thought of the telegram received that morning from her husband. 'Will try to meet train stop work busy stop if not at station get taxi stop.'

She stood by the little carving of the Virgin Mary in the alcove. 'It was this,' she said, her finger stroking the edge of the figure. 'Motherhood. I was here alone, and I stared at this, and I realized it reminded me of something, but I couldn't think what. And then I remembered, the painting above Finch's desk, the idealized image of motherhood, and I thought about the way Mr. Finch looked at Mrs. Collyer, and the last bit of the story fell into place. And that's when I saw that it was all so much more simple than anyone had realized.'

At her side, Kurt was gazing at the statue, and murmuring. She heard the words, repeated. '... pray for us sinners, now and at the hour of our death ...'

Quentin was standing close to him.

'... Holy Mary Mother of God ...' Kurt's voice was a low whisper.

'Kurt,' Quentin said.

'Theodore …' Kurt's eyes were dark with feeling, as he looked at Quentin.

'Kurt – it's over. The only person who needs to forgive you, is you.'

Kurt touched the clasped hands of the Virgin.

'Theo is at peace,' Quentin said. 'And his work lives on.'

Both men turned towards the fireplace, to the gap on the wall where the Antigone painting had once hung.

Kurt grasped Quentin's hand, and smiled.

They left the shadows of the hallway. Quentin pushed open the creaking door and all three came out into the summer sunshine. They walked down the steps to the Buick, climbed in, Quentin driving once more. The roof was down, and they shouted to make themselves heard above the wind, laughing as the sea air battered at their faces.

Quentin pulled up at the drive of the hotel. Kurt jumped out, held the door open for Agatha with an elaborate bow, smiling, touching his imaginary cap, then climbed back in next to Quentin, who revved away towards the car park.

Agatha's feet scrunched along the gravel as she approached the front door.

Nora was sitting on the wall, a book on her lap, her legs swinging against the smooth sandstone of the steps, the cascades of rhododendrons echoed in her bright silk dress, the ribbon of her straw hat.

'Oh, there you are,' she smiled. She patted the wall, and Agatha joined her there.

'Do you know,' Nora smiled, closed her novel, 'I went to visit him, this morning. Mr. Finch. He's in the police cells at Camborne. That nice Sergeant drove me over. Only just got back.' She shifted her legs on the wall. 'You see, all night I was thinking about him. Didn't sleep a wink. It is such an extraordinary thing to happen, that someone might think that about me, and about my husband, and that they might do something like that, something so very, very wrong ... terribly wrong. I didn't know what to think. So I thought, I must go and see him.'

Agatha rested her feet against the steps.

'I felt I should say something,' Mrs. Collyer continued. 'The man says he loves me, after all. So, I told him, that perhaps I might wait for him. Do you know what he said? He said, it was enough for him that I should be loved. He told me to go back to my life, to find happiness. He said, you're not to tie yourself up to another man's unhappiness, not again. He said he always knew that I would be a contented wife and a blissful mother, that was the word he used, "blissful" – and now it was time it should come true. Isn't that marvellous?' Her eyes sparkled. 'It is odd how well he seems to know me. It's as if he knows me far better than Frederick ever did. But the sad thing is, that even if I had met Mr. Finch, when I was free, and young ...' She shook her pretty curls. 'Oh dear, it sounds such a terrible thing to say. But the thing is, Mrs. Christie, Mr. Finch isn't someone I could ever have loved. Sweet as he is. There's something so soldierly about him. I don't mean that unkindly, but … some of these men, you just feel that somehow they're still fighting a war. You feel they'd be happier still in their barracks, still in uniform. As if it's shaped them, somehow.'

Agatha nodded. A sudden image of Archie, in his squadron-leader colours, proud, stiff-backed. And silent.

Nora swung her legs against the wall. 'Well, it is quite extraordinary. The sort of thing you read about in newspapers, isn't it, those little snippets when you think, don't other people have strange lives.'

'What will you do now?'

Nora smiled her sweet smile. 'I don't know. I really don't. My brother Peter is coming to drive me home, he's on his way. I told him all about it, I spoke to him on the Camborne telephone, the nice Sergeant arranged it for me. And Peter said he'd tell his friend James, and now it turns out they're both motoring down to collect me. They'll be here soon. That's why I thought I'd sit out here and wait for them, although if they take any longer I'll be wanting some lunch. And look, here comes Mr. Farrar and his friend from the big house.' She laughed, gaily, as Kurt and Quentin strolled round to the front door, inviting the ladies to join them for lunch, 'Sea trout, apparently,' Kurt laughed, 'freshly caught …'

But Nora insisted on staying on the wall just for a bit longer, 'This lovely sunshine is so health-giving …'

Agatha left her there, and followed Kurt and Quentin into the hotel.

*

Lunch had the atmosphere of a family meal. The Scottish ladies were louder, Blanche laughed gaily, Tyndall and Frau Adler sat together as if playing host. But there was a gap where Mr. Finch should have been, as if a major bit of clockwork was missing, so that somehow the salad seemed limp, the fish arrived after a long delay, the cutlery was chaotically placed. Oliver too, was subdued, waiting on tables. As he passed Frau Adler she put a maternal arm around him, murmured a few words, and he seemed to brighten.

At dessert, Tyndall approached Agatha's table. He reached out and grasped her hand. 'Don't suppose we'll meet again.' His voice was gruff. 'Wanted to say thank you.'

'Really, I did nothing ...'

'No, no –' he shook his head – 'seeing beyond the surface,' he said. 'That's what you did. Saved the day. For all of us.' He glanced across at Lillian, who flashed a warm smile. 'And here's Mrs. Collyer coming to say goodbye,' he went on. 'Her brother is taking care of her. Good thing too, I say.'

Nora was smiling as she crossed the dining room, with two young men behind her. One had the same soft blonde hair, the same pale eyes – 'Peter, come and meet Mrs. Christie, oh, do come and say hello, and you James, Mrs. Christie, this is James Wilkinson ...'

James had a warm dark smile, behind bookish spectacles. Hands were shaken, acknowledgements made.

'I am thrilled to meet you, Mrs. Christie,' James said. 'Had I thought of it, I'd have brought one of your wonderful books for you to personally inscribe.'

There was teasing, laughter, promises that she'd send him her next one, 'another masterwork, I don't doubt,' he'd said. Then the trio had tripped away, all set for luggage to be loaded, shawls to be fastened, hats to be pinned, ready for the long drive home.

*

Later Agatha went to her room to pack. The afternoon weather had remained settled. From her balcony she could see the rhododendrons basking in the afternoon sun, a blaze of colour against the neat green lawns.

On her desk lay her notebooks. She turned the pages, thinking about the Captain and his love for Martha Hobbes. She imagined herself, next day, alighting from the train, looking around her for Archie. Would she glimpse him, through the crowds and steam? Or would he see her first, and stride along the platform towards her?

She picked up her pen.

The old grey sundial was waiting in the rose garden. She looked at her handwriting on the page.

Or perhaps not the sundial. Perhaps the Captain and Martha could have their final declaration of love in a busy railway terminus, amidst the noise and smoke, a heart-warming reunion just when all seemed lost, and he can declare his love for her in all the hustle and bustle …

Tomorrow, she thought. Tomorrow I will go home.

She imagined stepping down from the train compartment. She imagined her husband's arms around her, their murmured words of delight at being once more together.

She remembered his telegram.

"Work busy. Stop. If not at station get taxi. Stop."

She stared at the page. Then she closed her notebook shut. She put down her pen, picked up her hat, left the hotel.

*

The sea was dazzling emerald, the coastal track golden with gorse, with swooping skylark song.

The shipwreck was deserted, lifeless.

She descended the track towards it.

She was aware of the clomp of feet on its tilted, half-rotten deck, of boots on the broken steps. Bosun Walker came into view.

'Hulloah,' he said. 'A last visit?'

She nodded.

'All of you leaving us now,' he said. 'Now the mystery is over.' He gave the hull an affectionate pat. 'Even though this mystery here is only just beginning.'

'It is?'

'Oh yes.' He leaned towards her, his gruff voice almost a whisper. 'We found something, at last. Well, the lads did. I wasn't here. Last night, they were out on the wall, drinking, as they do, and they heard singing. The moon was up, and they saw someone on the ship here. So, they came over, thought it was one of the village girls playing tricks – they could see her below decks, just there in the hold.

Johnny Beasley, he was telling me, she had a floating white dress, though one of the other lads said it wasn't white and it wasn't floating, and one of them said she was barefoot, and then one of the others said, no, clogs she was wearing, he heard their knock against the steps ... anyways, they chased her into the hold – and she'd gone. Vanished, they said. But they could still hear the singing, a sweet still voice mourning for her sailor man. And then that went too. But where she'd been, there was something. An ornamental casket, like a large jewellery box, just sitting there. We'd looked and looked, we'd stripped everything away, as you know. The lads were spooked, to be honest. They picked it up, carried it to shore. They were scared, not that they'd tell me, but they wouldn't open it. They waited for me, this morning. So we all opened it. And look.'

He led her round to the side of the wreck. A makeshift table had been set up, and on it stood a dark, weathered wooden box. Agatha could see its rusted clasp, the remnants of ornamental carving.

He bent to open it. 'And look what was inside.'

With great care, he lifted out what appeared to be a shoe. A delicate, ladies shoe.

'Leather,' he said. 'It can survive quite well, in some conditions.'

The shoe was golden yellow, punched with lace holes. It had a tapered toe and a small heel.

'Italian,' Ted Walker said. 'You can just make out the writing inside.'

Agatha looked at the shoe, then at him. 'The ghost story,' she said. 'Young Tilly waiting for her sailor.'

He gave a reluctant smile. 'That's what the lads were saying, this morning. The shoes brought back from Italy by the sailor-boy.' He shrugged. 'Like I said – a whole new story just starting here.'

'I wonder what happened to the other shoe,' Agatha said.

'There you are.' Bosun Walker smiled at her. 'You're the story-teller. You can start from there.' He placed the shoe carefully back into the casket.

She smiled. 'I may have enough of my own stories,' she said.

They turned away from the ship, away from the lapping waves.

'What will happen to it all?' Agatha asked.

'The museum in Camborne is keen on the shoe,' he said. 'Word's got out – we've already had those press-men down,' he said.

'And the ship?'

He turned back and surveyed the wreck. The charcoal lines seemed to shine, washed by sea water and sunlight.

'She belongs back there,' he said, pointing out to sea. 'She made her home in the depths,' he said. 'She should go back there.'

'Will the museum let you?' she asked.

He smiled. 'Probably not,' he said. 'Too many stories to tell.' He turned to her. 'Not that they'll ever get to the true story. That's lost in the depths too.' He held out his hand. 'It's been a pleasure meeting you, Mrs. Christie.'

She shook the offered hand, agreed that it had, indeed, been a pleasure.

'If you ever want to write a story set at sea, you know who to ask.' He touched his hat, gave a wave, headed away from her along the beach towards the sea wall. The villagers had gathered once more, and Agatha could hear fragments of song, snatches of music lost in the wind.

*

It was the ending of the day. Agatha left the beach and walked away, back up to the track.

Kurt was standing on the path, in the late afternoon sunlight.

'You had the same thought as me,' he said. 'To say farewell to the Lady Leona.'

He fell into step beside her, as they headed back to the hotel.

'That man they call the Bosun says the story isn't over,' Agatha said. 'They've found a casket after all. Late last night. Just sitting in the stairs by the hold.'

'Well, well,' he said. 'The casket promised to the ghostly maid?'

'Apparently so.'

'Complete with perfect leather shoes?'

'Well, that's the odd thing. There was a shoe, yes. One, single woman's shoe.'

'Heavens. In wonderful condition?'

'It's not bad,' she said. 'But the Boson says leather can do quite well in sea water.'

'Just the one,' Kurt said.

She nodded.

'Ah well.' Kurt paused, looked out to sea. 'Perhaps that's the problem with real life,' he said. 'That the story never quite comes out right. Never a perfect resolution. Unlike your story,' he added, turning to Agatha with a smile.

She turned to him. 'When you waited all night, at Langlands, in the old rose garden with a stone bench – did it have a sundial?'

He turned to her with a look of surprise. 'An old stone sundial. How did you know? It's a private garden – I had to shin up a fence just to get into it.'

She smiled. 'Sometimes a fictional story can come true.'

He laughed. His gaze turned back towards the sea. The shipwreck was a curve of black lines against the lowering sun. 'I might paint it,' he said. 'Those dark arcs against that pink light, the sea reflected...'

She glanced at him, looked back towards the ship.

He spoke again. 'Quentin says painting is like breathing. For me. That's what he says. He says painting, it's my vocation. For all these years it's as if I haven't been breathing.' He looked at her. 'Perhaps it's the same for you, telling a story. Resolving things. No doubt your romance will have a happy ending too.'

She thought about the pages heaped upon the table by the window. 'I think,' she said, 'I think you were right all along. I shan't write about love.'

'About death, then?' He raised an eyebrow.

She looked up at him. 'No, Mr. Farrar. I shall write what I always write. About the unmasking of a murderer, and the safeguarding of the innocent.'

'And will the butler have done it, Mrs. Christie?'

She smiled. 'What do you think, Mr. Farrar?'

He laughed. Beyond them lay the shimmering horizon, the white-flecked waves. A last look at the glitter of the sands, the pastel-painted walls of the nestling village. Then, they turned and walked back along the coastal track, towards the hotel.

Acknowledgements

Quotes from Antigone, from 'The Tragedies of Sophocles', translated by R. C Jebb, Cambridge University Press, 1904.

My characters are all fictional, but for more about the camoufleurs, see 'The Neglected Majority: "Les Camoufleurs," Art History, and World War I ' by Elizabeth Louise Kahn, 1984

Folk song lyrics adapted from traditional English folk song, 'Just as the Tide was Flowing.'

I wish to thank the staff of the British Library.

25171338R00101

Printed in Great Britain
by Amazon